'That's crazy,' he said, avoiding her gaze.

'Oh? You mean you might turn out to be a good guy after all?'

'I'm no saint,' he warned her.

She surprised him by reaching up to touch his cheek with her finger. 'What are you, then?'

She was too close, too tempting. Moving on reflex, he grabbed her by the hair at the back of her head and forced her face an inch from his own. 'I'm probably harder and rougher and less refined than any man you've ever been with, Charlie,' he told her, his voice a low rumble in his throat. 'Don't take this lightly.'

'I take you very seriously,' she told him softly, her voice pulsing with the excitement he was rousing in her blood. 'You are the most serious thing that has happened to me in a long time.'

Dear Reader,

Welcome! Feet aching from tramping round those January sales? Fingers numb from the bite of winter winds? Well, take the time to relax and warm up with this month's Desires...

January's MAN OF THE MONTH is *The Stardust Cowboy* by Anne McAllister—sparks are flying and a little boy is wishing for a dream to come true...

Alexandra Sellers begins a new trilogy, the SONS OF THE DESERT. In this month's book, the first instalment—*Sheikh's Ransom*—we find arrogant and sexy Prince Karim becoming more than fond of captive Caroline. And in the fourth part of the FOLLOW THAT BABY series we celebrate the New Year with a rags-to-riches tale in Christie Ridgway's *The Millionaire and the Pregnant Pauper*.

The CUTLER FAMILY saga continues with Marie Ferrarella's *A Match for Morgan*. Wedding bells are in the air but will they be ringing for Morgan?

In Kathryn Taylor's *The Scandalous Heiress*, Clayton Reese has his work cut out—he's trying to discover whether Mikki is con artist or wronged heiress *and* hold on to his heart... Finally, Raye Morgan delivers *Secret Dad*, where 'Charlie Smith' gets to pretend to be married to rugged mercenary Denver McCaine...lucky woman!

Enjoy yourself,

The Editors

Secret Dad

RAYE MORGAN

SILHOUETTE

DESIRE®

*Silhouette, Silhouette Desire and Colophon
are registered trademarks of Harlequin Books S.A.,
used under licence.*

*First published in Great Britain 2000
Silhouette Books, Eton House, 18-24 Paradise Road,
Richmond, Surrey TW9 1SR*

© Helen Conrad 1999

ISBN 0 373 76199 6

22-0001

*Printed and bound in Spain
by Litografia Rosés S.A., Barcelona*

RAYE MORGAN

favours settings in the West of the USA, which is where she has spent most of her life. She admits to a penchant for Western heroes, believing that whether he's a rugged outdoors-man or a smooth city sophisticate, he tends to have a streak of wildness that the romantic heroine can't resist taming. She's been married to one of those Western men for twenty years and is busy raising four more in her Southern California home.

Prologue

Robbie lifted his tousled head and listened. He could hear his mother talking and laughing softly with friends in the next room. The sound of her voice filled his almost-six-year-old heart with satisfaction and he snuggled down into his thick, soft covers, holding his teddy bear. He loved his mom.

"But where's your dad?" his friend Billy had asked insistently that afternoon when they were playing in the mud at the edge of the lake. "Where is he, huh?"

He frowned, remembering. It made him feel funny and hollow inside to think about it. Billy had a dad. He was big and loud and he took Billy fishing on Sunday afternoons. You were supposed to have a dad. Where was his dad?

His mother had said just tonight, "Your birthday is coming up, Robbie. Better start thinking about what you're going to wish for."

Could you wish for a dad for your birthday? He wasn't sure. He didn't want to say anything to his mom. He hated it when she looked sad and something told him asking for a dad would make her sad. So he would have to ask someone else.

Putting his hands together, he squeezed his eyes tightly shut and whispered, "Please, please. Could you bring me a dad? I promise I'll sweep the porch every day and brush my teeth every night. So could you? Could you make him sort of big? I really, really need him." He opened his eyes, then quickly closed them again, because he'd almost forgotten. "Thank you," he added quickly. "Thank you very much. And God bless Mom."

One

Denver McCaine winced as he climbed the trail to the cabin he'd rented for the month. His bruised, broken and thirty-eight-year-old body was rebelling, and he didn't blame it. He'd wanted something remote, but if he'd known the cabin was going to be this hard to get to, he would have opted for something closer to the edge of the water.

"Go stay at Big Tree Lakes," his coordinator, Josh Hoya had advised him. "You've had three rough assignments in a row. You're not going to make it through another one without taking some time to heal."

The casual onlooker might have thought Josh compassionate, but Denver knew better. Josh just wanted him ready for his next mission, and he wanted him in shape, just in case Denver had to pull the usual dangerous stunts he'd become known for during his almost twenty years as a government agent. But for the first time, Denver wasn't sure he was going to be back when his R and R was over. For the first time, he felt a certain lack of will he'd never experienced before.

"You're getting old," he told himself, stopping to rest with his hand jammed against the rough bark of a pine to hold himself up. It might be time to consider changing to a desk job.

But that made him grin. A desk job—that would never happen. It just wasn't his style. Still, this climb was destroying his right knee. He looked around for a better way to make it up to the cabin and his eye fell on an old streambed. That might give him better footing. He walked gingerly toward the rocky gully, cursing the foreign government soldier who had taken a whack at his leg with the butt of a rifle just three weeks ago—and the sniper who had put a bullet into his backside. All in all, he felt just this side of broken.

But he should have been paying attention to where he was placing his feet rather than cataloguing his pains. One misstep, then another, and he was falling, reaching out to try to catch himself on brush that came away in his hand, sliding down into the streambed on his back, wedged in between two boulders and twisted so that he knew right away it was going to be very difficult for him to get back up on his own.

A wave of pain swept over him and he closed his eyes for a moment, waiting for it to pass so that he could think straight. In the meantime, he uttered every curse word he knew, and some he'd only read in ancient books. This was so stupid, so avoidable. "See," he muttered darkly to himself. "More evidence you're losing your edge." He never made mistakes like this. What the hell was the matter with him?

Once he felt his strength coming back, he tried to leverage himself up into a sitting position, but he couldn't get the traction he needed. His right leg was gone, completely unusable, and without it, he didn't know how he was going to get up again.

He lay there, unbelieving, stream water soaking his pants. He was helpless. He—Denver McCaine, government agent, adventurer, sometime mercenary rescuer of damsels in distress, defender of the weak, the man who went where wise men feared to tread—here he was, flat on his back like a damn turtle. If he hadn't felt so completely humiliated, he might have laughed.

"Hold on. I'm coming."

The voice was female and he groaned. No woman should ever see him like this. This was not the face he usually presented to the world.

She came scrambling over the bank and toward him.

"Are you hurt? Do I dare move you? Or should I run into town and get a doctor?"

At first all he saw was a swirl of blond hair slashing through the sunlight above him, but as she bent over him, her face began to take shape and come into focus.

"I'm not really hurt," he said gruffly, wondering just how he was going to explain. "I mean, I'm hurt, but it's from an earlier incident. This isn't bodily injury. It is, however, a definite wound to the spirit."

She laughed softly, not taking him at his word as she quickly and gently tested his limbs for broken bones. "You seem to be okay," she said, taking his hand. "You want to help me pull you up? I think I can do it."

She set her feet against the rocks and locked her knees, tensing, and he set his jaw and willed her maneuver to work. Though she had to strain beyond what she'd expected, she soon had him back in a sitting position and out from between the two boulders.

"There," she said, smiling at him and brushing her hands together as though she felt it had been a job well done. "How are you feeling?"

He didn't answer. If he had been a normal man, his jaw might have dropped. But since he was a well-trained saboteur and warrior, he automatically hid his reaction to seeing her face-to-face. However, hiding was one thing—actually producing friendly chitchat was another. He was silent much too long for comfort, staring at her.

But he needed the time to soak in the vision before him, because she was not a stranger. This was a woman he knew. He remembered her from years before. Hers was not a face that was easy to forget. He placed her immediately, remembering the private boarding school he'd scrimped and saved and put his life on the line to send his little sister to. This woman had been his sister's roommate, and everything about her had been indelibly branded into his brain.

"Uh…are you sure you're okay?" she asked him, growing a bit anxious at the silence and searching his face.

He nodded, still struck dumb. She was more beautiful than ever, her hair a floating cloak the color of corn silk, her huge violet eyes soft as velvet, her hands fluttering like small birds. She wore white shorts and a blue halter top and her skin looked like butter, like cream, so smooth he could almost taste it. At first glance, she could still have been a girl, but another look showed a depth of experience in her sultry eyes. The lovely girl he'd admired years ago had turned into a woman.

"My name is Charlie Smith," she said sunnily.

"The hell it is," he muttered, surprised. Adrianna Charlyne Chandler was more like it.

"What?" she asked brightly, puzzled by him.

But he shook his head and didn't repeat it, and she seemed to assume he was in pain from the sympathetic look on her face.

Charlie Smith indeed. That was a good one.

But wait. Suddenly he realized she must have gotten married since he knew her. After all, he told himself savagely, the rest of the world couldn't sit around waiting for his adolescent dreams to clear up like a bad case of acne. Of course she was married, probably to some handsome stockbroker who wore double-breasted suits and talked on his cell phone all day—some normal but very wealthy man whom she adored and who was as different from Denver as night was from day. That was the way things worked, and he didn't have to think very hard to know it might work that way for her.

"My name's Denver," he told her when he realized it was time to reciprocate. "Denver, uh…Smith."

She laughed, delighted. "Not really? Isn't that a scream? You're a Smith, too?"

He nodded, frowning slightly and wondering if her name was as phony as his. He'd rented the cabin under the name of D. Smith, more out of force of habit than anything else. The years had taught him to go incognito whenever possible, because his line of work was one that cultivated enemies and you couldn't be too careful. And Smith was about as anonymous as you could get.

"What a coincidence," she said, looking as though that really tickled her.

"Yeah," he replied, hoping she didn't catch the sarcasm in his tone. He was going to have to watch that. Sarcasm was all very well in his line of work, but it wouldn't do around ladies like this.

He rose a little shakily and tried to walk, but the right knee was having none of it. It collapsed under him and she had to reach out quickly to help him regain his balance.

"Bad luck," she murmured. "You're not going to get far on that leg, are you?"

He didn't answer. He was too busy experiencing the feel of her hands and taking in her honey scent as she helped him sit back down on a flat rock. He'd never been this close to her before. In fact, he didn't think he'd ever spoken directly to her before. But he had certainly been aware of her existence.

"Where are you staying?" she asked him, standing over him with her hands on her hips.

He gestured in the direction of his cabin up the steep side of the hill.

She looked from the rugged terrain to his leg and shook her head. "You're not going to make it up there under your own steam, that's a cinch. We'd better call for a paramedic."

"No," he said quickly. "I can handle it by myself."

She gazed at him frankly. "No, you can't. Listen, my cabin's not far, and it's all downhill from here. You'd better come and rest there until we figure out what to do."

"Forget it." Rising, he lurched forward, almost falling again.

She was there in a flash, holding his arm, acting as his support. "Come on, tough guy. You're coming home with me."

He looked down into her mass of shiny hair. "Your husband…"

She stiffened. "I don't have a husband. Only one little five-year-old boy, who is going to be thrilled to see you. Come on."

He hesitated but she wasn't taking no for an answer, and he'd lost the will to fight for the moment. His leg felt pretty bad. She was probably right. And for the first time since his mother had died, he meekly did what a woman told him to do.

Two

Charlie's arm, stabilizing Denver, was sure and steady. She was stronger than she looked. He gritted his teeth and avoided her eyes. He wasn't used to accepting this sort of help from anyone, and to think that he was dependent on this slender slip of a woman really stuck in his craw. But every time he tried to put any weight on his bad leg, the pain shot through him like the slash of a knife. There was no help for it. He was stuck with the situation, at least for now.

The going was slow at first, but once they got the hang of it, they started to move. His wet slacks slapped against his legs, getting colder and colder in the breeze. He felt very aggrieved. His life wasn't supposed to go like this.

"Here we go," she told him brightly, flashing him a smile. "My cabin's just a little further. There it is, just above the boat ramp by the lake."

He looked up and saw an austere-looking cabin just ahead. "That one?"

"No, that one belongs to my friend Margo and her husband." Charlie grinned. "If she's watching, I'm sure she's on the phone to everyone we know. This must look quite a sight to her." She nodded further on. "That's my cabin, just to the left."

He could tell right away that she'd lived in the little bungalow for some time. There were flowers on vines twining everywhere, in pots, creeping up porch posts, in beds alongside the path to the front door. Tiny buds of yellow and lavender and pink and white peeked from under leaves in every direction. It looked like a damn fairy-tale cottage or something equally sappy and that didn't soften his mood. The hand-painted wooden sign over the door didn't help either. Welcome Home, it said.

Home. Funny how that word resonated, even when you didn't have a home.

"Aren't you being a little free with your welcome?" he grumbled, gesturing toward the sign as he hobbled onto her porch. "After all, you never know who might decide to take you up on it." He glanced at her, noting the way she was biting her lower lip as she struggled to help him through her doorway. "Can't be too careful these days," he added to cover up his own embarrassment at his predicament.

She didn't respond, and once inside, he blinked, adjusting his vision to the interior gloom after the bright light outside. The place looked like more of the same cheerfulness he'd encountered on the porch—a clutter of handmade wall items, quilted throw comforters and copper pots and pans stacked neatly at the end of the breakfast bar. He might have said it looked like a

Snow White cottage waiting for the Seven Dwarfs to come whistling in from the mines, except there wasn't a sign that anyone masculine had ever been in the place. Anyone over five years old, at any rate.

For some reason, that annoyed him even more, and he frowned, leaning against the back of a wooden chair while she got the couch ready for him, fluffing pillows and moving a small stack of magazines. As she leaned down to work, her blond hair swung about her face, catching the light from the window. Her halter top gaped, showing a generous measure of flesh and exposing breasts just the size he liked them. He hadn't remembered her with that much of a figure, but she certainly had made up for lost time since he'd seen her last.

"Okay, Mr. Smith," she said brightly, turning toward him. "Give me your arm. We'll get you settled on the couch."

"I can handle it," he said, pulling away from her and hobbling over on his own.

She watched him position himself to drop down on the cushion, and shrugged. "I'm going to call a doctor," she said, starting for the phone.

"No, you're not." There was an element of command in his voice that stopped her in her tracks. He levered himself down onto the couch, wincing. "I don't need a doctor." He glanced up and met her gaze. "But I'm going to need you. You're going to have to help me take my pants off."

Charlie's eyes widened and a bubble of laughter rose in her throat, but she managed to hold her composure. It was clear from his tone and from the look he threw in her direction that he thought the suggestion would shock her in some way. "You think I'm too prissy for a job like that, don't you?'' she accused him. ''Well, you just watch, mister.'' She came forward with no hesitation, her violet eyes challenging him. ''Here's a news flash. I take men's pants off all the time.''

Her hands were on his belt before his were, and he lay back against the pillows and let her work. She slipped the belt off and undid the button, then yanked the zipper down.

''You going to help at all?'' she asked him tartly.

He kept his mouth from curling but he couldn't keep the grin out of his eyes. ''I'll do my best,'' he said, and he braced himself on his elbows and lifted his hips so that she could tug the slacks down over his green plaid boxers and past his knees. Suddenly he wanted to hurry her along to get this over with before the evidence of how this was affecting him became all too obvious.

And it was affecting him. A hot, heavy pulse was beginning to beat in his veins. Feeling like this just wasn't right—not for her, the woman he'd idolized for years. Oh hell, face it. She was the woman he'd *lusted* after for years. The woman he'd never thought he would get anywhere near. And now—here he was. And she was taking off his pants.

''How's your shirt?'' she asked, shaking out the pants and laying them near the fireplace.

''Just a little wet around the edges,'' he said quickly. ''It's okay.''

She touched it and gave him a scornful look. ''Hand it over,'' she said cheerfully, turning to stoke her little fire. ''We might as well try, at least, to keep you from catching pneumonia.''

He pulled the shirt over his head and handed it to

her, grabbing a throw that lay along the back of the couch and covering his semi-naked body with it just as she turned back to him.

"Wait a minute," she said, sliding in to sit on the coffee table where she could have easy access to him. "I want to have a look at that leg."

"Hey, no—" he began, but her small hands were already pushing back the blanket and beginning to gently probe around the joint.

"I can't take the place of a doctor," she told him as she worked. "But I do know something about this." She glanced up and met his startled gaze. "I volunteer at the local hospital one day a week," she explained with a quick smile. "That's where I've been getting my practice at disrobing men."

"Oh." He couldn't think of anything else to say. There she was, her beautiful face clouded with intensity as she tested his leg, her gorgeous breasts moving in that flimsy blue halter top as she worked, her warm hands on his rough skin. A feeling very near despair came over him. He felt like a man drowning in pure gold. Too much of a good thing couldn't help but bring on disaster. Could it?

"I've had a lot of experience with sprains and breaks," she went on as she probed. "In the winter, we get a lot of skiers. And skiers get a lot of leg injuries."

He was speechless. He felt almost mesmerized by her touch on his leg, and he stared at her, heart thumping. What had happened? Had his fall taken him through the looking glass? Was this heaven or something? Was this woman an angel?

No. No angel's touch would have stirred his blood the way her hands did. He moved restlessly, hoping she wouldn't notice, and forcing himself to keep his mind from straying into forbidden territory. You weren't supposed to think about angels like that.

"No kidding," he responded lamely at last. "A candy-striper, huh?"

She nodded, a small frown of concentration puckering her brow as she evaluated his condition. He took a deep breath and tried counting backwards from a hundred, but he kept losing his place. All he could think about was Charlie, volunteer health worker, rescuer of damaged hikers. Angel or no angel, the woman seemed to be trying out for sainthood. Next she was going to tell him that she went around every morning and let wolves and foxes out of traps. Fed the starving. Let the homeless live on her porch. It was a bit much. He wasn't sure why, but he halfway resented her goodness.

Maybe it was because all this altruism didn't fit with the image he'd had of her years ago. She'd been lovely and appealing—but just as self-centered and snooty as most of the well-bred and overindulged girls at the private school where he'd seen her. Something had changed her. Either that, or she was putting up a very convincing front.

"I don't think anything is broken," she told him, still at work with her strong slender fingers. "But your cartilage is shot, isn't it? And your patella…"

"Ow," he muttered, jerking away as her hand found a raw nerve. His movement displaced the blanket and it slipped down off his chest. She reached automatically to straighten it for him, and he reached at the same time. She would have beaten him to it, but something stopped her, shocked her for a moment. He saw the stunned look in her eyes and he knew what it

was. The blanket had uncovered the huge, jagged scar
on his chest. She'd seen it, and now she was going to
draw away in horror. It happened every time.

He pulled the blanket up and then he waited for it,
holding his breath, and the tension grew tight as a
drum. He forced himself to look into her eyes. If he
saw even a hint of pity there...

"I bet you'll have plenty of stories to tell your
grandchildren," she said lightly, reaching to cover his
scarred leg as well. "You certainly seem to carry
around a lot of reminders of adventures past."

He gazed at her in wonder as she rose above him.
No one had ever come that close to saying exactly the
right thing before.

She leaned over him, tucking in the blanket, and as
she did, the halter top gapped again, showing everything but the very tips of her breasts, and her hair slid
down like a fragrant veil, brushing his face, and the
world seemed to be spinning out of control. Like a
man in a dream, he reached out, acting on pure instinct, and grabbed her wrist, pulling her closer. She
was so soft, so light, and desire for her swept through
him like a surge in the sea. She didn't try to pull away.
She looked startled, but not afraid. She stared into his
gaze, her face only inches from his, and he searched
her violet eyes, but he couldn't read her real reaction.
Still, he knew he could kiss her easily. It would take
only a slight tug to pull her down on top of him and
take her mouth with his. The urge to do it choked in
his throat.

But he couldn't. This wasn't any woman he'd
picked up in the forest on an afternoon's walk. This
was Charlyne Chandler, for God's sake. What the hell
did he think he was doing?

He released her without saying a word, and she drew back slowly. Was that regret he caught in her gaze? Or maybe disgust? He couldn't tell. And maybe he didn't even want to know.

"You shouldn't do that," he told her softly as she sat back on the coffee table.

"Do what?" she asked, brushing the hair back away from her face.

He watched her with narrowed eyes. "When a man's been out on the desert for a few days, you shouldn't wave a glass of water in front of him unless you're going to let him take a drink." He winced once the words were out of his mouth. It had seemed like a good metaphor when he'd thought of it, but out loud, it sounded very silly. He looked at her, wondering what she thought.

She stared at him for a long moment, and then she burst into laughter, holding her arms in close and rocking with it. "That's the most ridiculous thing I've ever heard," she said.

He shrugged, suppressing a smile himself. "I'm just warning you. A man can only take so much temptation."

"You're not a regular man," she protested, rising from the table. "You're a wounded man."

"I'd have to be a dead man not to react to—"

"Okay, okay," she said quickly, not wanting him to describe what he was looking at. But she began to edge away from him. "Let me just slosh my way to my room and change into something else. Like a raincoat, maybe." Turning, she left the room.

He lay back and berated himself. Well, that was just great. Now he'd offended her. He hadn't meant to do that. He swore under his breath. He hadn't meant to end up on a woman's couch today, but here he was. And the sooner he got out of here the better.

She was back in a moment, and he noticed she'd changed her clothes. The air had turned chilly, unfortunately, and she'd put on jeans and a long-sleeved shirt. There would be no more luscious vistas of smooth, clear skin, no more glimpses of cleavage. In a way, it was almost a relief. Maybe now the charged atmosphere would calm down a little.

She dropped to the floor in front of the embers that filled her fireplace and began to shove the glowing coals with a poker. He watched as she put on a log, stirred the ashes, and got a few flames to flicker at the wood. For just a moment he was tempted to give her advice on her technique, but he caught himself just in time.

But then he began to wonder—what was she doing here in these primitive surroundings? The Charlyne he remembered belonged in mansions, with graceful staircases climbing to the sky and gardeners trimming the roses and a woman who took your coat when you came in. This was a whole new side of her and he wondered where it had come from.

She went on talking, chatting about simple things, not expecting a response from him, and to his surprise, he was relaxing, feeling almost comfortable. She had a knack. He was soothed, just beginning to get sleepy, when there was a scratching sound, and a short bark from outside, and she rose with a smile.

"And now you're about to meet the reason I don't feel unsafe in this place," she told him as she went toward the sound. "Here you go." She threw open the door. "Meet Sabrina."

Sabrina was a dark husky, big and furry and very,

very curious. She knew Denver was there right away and raced to the couch, her nails scratching on the wood floor.

"Hold it, girl," Charlie cried, coming after her quickly. "Sabrina has been known to take exception to some men who have been in this house," she added, watching the dog and the man meet. "She's never actually bitten anyone, but you never know."

But the big dog didn't hesitate. Rising up on her hind legs, she placed her paws right on Denver's chest and began to sniff him all over. Charlie made a move as though to pull her back, but Denver reached up and gave her a rough caress, letting Charlie know he was perfectly willing to put up with Sabrina's test. The dog let out a sharp bark, wagged her tail twice, and settled back down, almost seeming to give Charlie a nod as she went. Charlie laughed.

"You big old faker," she told her pet, giving her a rub on the top of her head as she passed.

Denver watched her go. "Nice dog," he said. "She's got eyes like an old Indian sage. Like she's carrying around the wisdom of the ages."

Charlie shook her head. "Don't let her fool you. She's just a puppy at heart." Moving quickly, she began picking things up, making small talk as she went.

He was hearing the sound of her voice more than the words. It was like music. She went into the kitchen and began fixing something. He assumed it was for dinner, though it was still early. He stared into the fire and listened to her talk. Her voice was quick, just like her hands. The sound she made was light and sunny, like the song a perfect stream sang as it danced over polished stones. He closed his eyes for a moment. He could almost taste her.

There was a clattering of pans and the sound of water running. Now she was humming a lively tune. He had an urge to see her and he hunched himself up higher against the arm of the couch so that he could look across the room and into the kitchen.

"Is it really that much fun to cook?" he asked her as the humming went on and on.

She glanced up, as though astonished he was still there. "You'd be surprised," she said, laughing, her hair swinging about her shoulders.

"It does smell good," he admitted.

"Do you like pot roast?"

Pot roast. How many years had it been since he'd had good old homemade pot roast? His diet over the last few years had tended toward hamburgers or a taco grabbed on the fly—that, or the native cuisine of whatever country he was working in. Pot roast took a long time. Mothers made pot roast. It was the sort of dinner that had love cooked right into it—along with Sunday afternoons and going to church with the family.

He twitched. Where the hell had that picture come from? It didn't sound like any sort of life that he'd ever led. What happened? Were you born with some sort of stereotype in your head that you tried to live up to your entire life? Tried, and failed. Kind of a great eternal joke on humanity.

"I didn't realize that was such a hard question," she commented.

He looked up, at a loss for a moment. Then he remembered what she'd asked. "Uh...sure. I like pot roast."

"Good. I'm making plenty. You can have all you want."

It seemed he was expected to stay for dinner. Suddenly the prospect of a homemade meal was overwhelmingly seductive. He sat back and contemplated his luck. He knew he should go. But one good old pot roast dinner wouldn't hurt. Would it?

"You know," she said, coming out of the kitchen. "I really think you should go to the hospital."

He grimaced, shifting his leg. "What for?"

"They'll fix you right up, put you in a cast, make sure you're on the road to healing…"

He was shaking his head. "No. I'm not going to the hospital." He'd already spent too many weeks in the hospital this year. "I've had worse than this before. The human body has a capacity to heal all sorts of things on its own. And mine's had a lot of practice at it."

She gazed at him curiously, but didn't respond to what he'd said. "Okay, I guess I can't force you." Starting toward the door, she called back, "You'll have to hold the fort. I've got to go get Robbie. He gets out of school at three and…."

As though she knew this part by heart, Sabrina came running out of the back of the house to join her mistress. Charlie stopped at the door, her hand on the knob. "You'll be here when I get back, won't you?" she asked.

He looked at her. Her lips were curved into a slight smile and her eyes were alight with the question. Tiny wisps of blond hair flew around her lovely face. It was a good thing he'd learned to harden himself over the years. A weaker man wouldn't have been able to resist the temptingly engaging picture she presented.

"Sure, I'll be here," he told her gruffly. "Where the hell would I go?"

Her face changed and she straightened her shoulders, taking a couple of steps back toward where he lay. "Okay, I've been meaning to talk to you about that. When my son is around, I'd appreciate it if you would watch the swearing. You seem to do an awful lot of it, and I don't like it." She paused. "On the other hand, it's a free country. You can swear all you want. Only not around Robbie. That I won't allow."

She'd caught him off guard again. He hadn't realized he'd been getting that careless—like some mountain man who didn't know how to behave in civilized society. Great. Now he was so far gone he was swearing around a woman. He'd lived a tough life. He'd sworn a lot in his time. But he still had some old-fashioned values. He never used to swear around women and children. He was going to have to relearn that.

"Don't worry," he told her. "I'll watch it."

Her smile was back, as though she were glad he'd taken criticism so well. "I'd appreciate it," she said breezily, spinning back toward the exit. "It takes twenty minutes to get to Robbie's school. Twenty minutes back."

She didn't wait for an answer, and he didn't give one. He only stared after the closing door, wondering how he'd managed to end up here when all he'd come for was rest and relaxation. Something told him rest was going to be hard to find with Charlie around.

Three

_____

Charlie left her cabin and started toward town. Smoke was coming out of the chimney at Margo's place, so she was home. Charlie had a moment's unease, of wondering what the neighbors would think about her visitor, but she brushed it away. That was old thinking, from her past. She was a different person now.

She was a little late and she walked quickly, buoyed by some sort of sparkling in her veins. She didn't know what it was, but she had energy to burn today.

"Could it be because I've got a man on my couch?" she muttered to herself, then laughed aloud, making Sabrina run back and dash about her ankles to see what was so funny.

A man—a pretty common item for most women to have around. But not her. She'd avoided men for so many years now, she hardly knew how to handle one now that she had him. She'd had a man in her life

once before. He'd fathered her son. For that, she
would always be grateful. But he'd also made life even
more miserable than it had been before he came along
and she'd run as far and as fast as she could to get
away from him.

Some women were not meant to have a man. She'd
decided that must be the case a long time ago, and
that maybe she was one of them. Her experience with
marriage had been such a disaster, she knew she would
have a hard time risking it again. She'd been lucky to
have gotten away, lucky that no one had found her in
all these years. She and her son Robbie were together,
and that was all she needed. She couldn't imagine being any happier than she was right now.

So why had she brought the man home, like some
wounded puppy who needed ministering to? She
wasn't sure. She'd thought at first, just for a moment
or two, that he looked familiar. But that couldn't be.
The life she'd lived before she'd moved here hadn't
included men like Denver. Still, there was something
in his face—something slightly familiar and yet not.
Something that made her trust him, even though he'd
given her no real reason to do anything of the kind.

She knew that if she ever did pick a new man to
marry, it wouldn't be a man like Denver. If she got to
that point, she would be looking for a professional
man, someone solid and reassuring. Denver was too
rough, too…well, dangerous was a good word for it.
There was something a bit intimidating about him. She
had the feeling that he would do just about anything
for someone, if he cared enough.

And those scars on his body! Good grief. She shuddered, thinking about them. She'd seen enough at the
hospital to know those weren't football injuries. The

man had been knifed and shot and who knew what else? At some point in his life, he had obviously been involved in something very dangerous.

And then there was that moment when he'd taken hold of her wrist and pulled her close. She'd felt so strange—as though she'd almost been waiting for him to do it. She'd seen the raw hunger in his eyes and her heart had beat so loudly, she could hardly breathe. She'd thought he would kiss her. But it didn't happen, and she caught her breath now, thinking about it. Did she want that? Did she? Shaking her head, she pushed it away. She couldn't let herself dwell on that. It brought up too many conflicting emotions.

And the school was just ahead, a little wood frame building nestled in a clearing rimmed with ponderosa pine. The children were just coming out and she waved at Robbie, nodded and called greetings to a few friends, then he came barreling toward her and she reached down and caught her son up in her arms. She held him tightly, smelled his hair, felt the spirit that filled him, and thanked God for him one more time. Sometimes, life was good.

"We had worms," he told her happily.

"Worms?" She eased him to the ground and gazed at him in trepidation, hoping it wasn't a meal he was talking about.

He nodded, his eyes sparkling. "Big ones. They wiggled."

"Oh." Charlie was laughing again. "They wiggled, did they?"

"Uh-huh." He began to walk along beside her. "We watched them go into the ground and then we dug them up again."

"Lovely."

He scrunched up his face and looked at her from under a stray lock of hair. "Could I have a worm for a pet? Just a little one?"

Charlie hesitated. Worms as pets. Wonderful. "I'm afraid not, honey," she told him calmly. "Worms don't do real well in captivity." She winced as she saw the disappointment on his round face. "But you know what? I'll bet we have worms living right in our yard. Later on, maybe we could dig up some dirt and see."

"Could we?" He was happy again. "Great! When I find one I'm going to name him Cowabunga," he called as he ran off to chase Sabrina through the trees.

Charlie smiled. Being with Robbie always made her smile. He was the joy in her life—practically the reason she lived at this point. He was the only thing she'd taken with her when she ran away. He would be with her until he was grown and then she would finally be alone. But she didn't want to think about that. That day was a long way off—and this day was too beautiful for melancholy thoughts. Right now, her heart was light as a breeze.

Some days she picked Robbie up with her little motor scooter, carrying him home clinging to her waist as they roared over the bumps. But she liked best the days when they walked home together and he told her about what he'd learned. They were close in ways she'd never been with her own family, and that was just the way she'd planned it from the beginning. As far as she was concerned, her relationship with her son was a golden gift she would treasure and work to maintain. She would do almost anything to make sure it never got to be the way it had always been with her own mother.

For some reason, that made her think about Denver Smith, and before she could stop herself, she shivered with anticipation, then gasped at her own foolishness. "Wow," she whispered to herself as a bird cried in the tree above her. "The man really *is* dangerous, isn't he?" And that made her shiver again. She had a dangerous man in her living room and she could hardly wait to go be scared of him. What nonsense!

A giggle rose in her throat. What if her mother could see Denver, could know the way Charlie was reacting to him? She could see her mother's strong, handsome face grimacing in disgust.

"A hooligan!" she would say disapprovingly. "We don't invite hooligans into our home."

"No," Charlie said, laughing in a way she would never have laughed in front of the woman. "No, Mother. *You* don't. But *I* do. And that is one reason why I don't live with you any longer."

Brave words, she thought, sobering. Too bad she'd never be able to say them to her mother's face. Well, there was no question about it. The man *was* dangerous. She could see it in his eyes and in the evidence that scarred his body. You didn't end up with a body like that playing tennis at the club. She'd never dealt with a man who'd actually been shot before.

"No more shivering," she told herself firmly, and then her smile was back.

Robbie came skipping out of the trees and slowed to walk beside her.

"Mom, how come your eyes are sparkling?" he asked.

She looked down at him. "What?"

"Like stars." He nodded, gazing into them.

She laughed. "Oh, come on."

He wrinkled his tiny freckled nose, his blue eyes wise. "Do you have a surprise at home for me?" he asked carefully.

She sighed, shaking her head, delighted with him as usual. "How did you guess that?"

He shrugged. "Because of your eyes," he said sensibly. "Because you look like a surprise."

Laughing, she pulled him up into her arms and gave him a very loud kiss on his flushed cheek.

"Is it a rifle?" he asked hopefully.

"Robbie!" she cried, dropping him on his feet again. "No, it's not a rifle. And it never will be, you can count on that. I don't think you should have a rifle. And I wish you would stop asking for one all the time."

He took her small lecture patiently, then got back to business right away. "Then what kind of surprise is it?" he asked, pulling further away so that he could skip along beside her.

"It's not a toy surprise, either," she warned him. "More of a people-to-people surprise."

He thought about that for a moment, frowning then shook his head and asked, "What does that mean?"

"You just wait. You'll see."

His eyes widened and he started to ask something else, but he quickly thought better of it, and instead put his head down and began to walk on ahead as fast as he could, with Sabrina dancing beside him, watching for something to chase. But Robbie wasn't interested in the forest any longer. He seemed to be intent on getting home.

Charlie shook her head, watching him. She so often worried that it wasn't fair to try to raise him all alone, that he really needed a dad in his life. That was something she couldn't give him. The thought of going out and trying to find a man to take over that role made her cringe. Unfortunately, she was afraid Robbie was going to have to grow up without a father around. Not an ideal situation, but the best she could do.

She hoped he would like having Denver stay for dinner. There hadn't often been a man in their house lately. Now and then she invited Robbie's friend Billy to come to a meal and bring his parents. She had noted the way Robbie hung on every word Billy's father uttered, and followed him with his eyes at all times. It was obvious how much her son longed for a dad of his own. She wasn't sure what he would make of Denver, but she was pretty sure their visitor was made from the mold every little boy liked to think of his father as being from. That was the best she could do for him, it seemed—occasional and temporary male influences in his life.

Robbie was walking faster and faster and she almost had to run to catch up to him. He pulled her by the hand and she laughed as he forced her to trot, with Sabrina dashing around them and barking. In no time at all, they were home, running up the porch steps and bursting in through the front door.

The house seemed too still and she looked around quickly, her gaze darting from the couch to the kitchen and back again. The blanket lay neatly folded on the table. The fire had just about gone out. There was no sign of him. He was gone.

Something lurched inside her but she didn't stop to analyze why. He was gone and she was disappointed, but she wasn't going to let it show.

Robbie looked around too, puzzled. ''Where is it, Mom? I can't find the surprise.''

"I'm sorry, honey," she told him, letting her fingertips trail along the back of the couch where Denver had been when she'd last seen him, remembering how big and rough he'd looked when she'd had him there. "I guess your surprise has sort of…disappeared."

He was gone. The disappointment welled up in her like a thundercloud pouring over the tips of the mountain range on a summer day. She'd brought home a lost creature, tended to him, grown to rather like him, and now he was gone. That left an empty spot in her soul.

The sound of something outside caught her attention. There was a noise from out back, a thump, the sound of an ax against wood. She stopped, frowning, and suddenly she realized it was made by someone chopping firewood. Her heart leaped up but she didn't let herself notice that. Instead, she ran to the window and looked out. He wasn't gone after all. There he was, ax in hand, chopping wood. That thing that had lurched inside her rose again, rose and poured something warm and sweet through her body, and she grinned, feeling suddenly light as air.

"Or maybe not," she told her son, tousling his hair as she passed him on her way outside. "Let me go see." She stepped quickly to the back door.

There he was, swinging an ax in a very unbalanced manner, his hair shining in the sun. Throwing open the door, she ran out.

"What are you doing?" she cried out as she neared him. "Will you cut that out?"

He turned and nodded to greet her. "That's exactly what I'm trying to do," he told her, setting himself and taking another swing.

"You are in no condition to be doing something

like this," she said, frowning as he staggered back from the momentum of the ax. Reaching out, she put a hand on his arm, and he didn't pull away, but he stiffened, and she knew he didn't want her doing that. Quickly, she pulled her hand back.

"Come on in and sit down," she said quickly. "We'll be eating soon."

He was leaning against the sawhorse that held the wood in place and it was obvious he was going to have to take her suggestion, whether he wanted to or not. "I'm actually doing fine," he protested, though he didn't look it. "The leg is getting back to normal. Really, I'm okay."

She frowned, not buying it. "Let's go have dinner," she said again.

He shifted his weight and glanced at her, stalling for time. "Dinner already?" he said. "Isn't it a little early for that?"

"We have to eat early. I have to be at work at five."

He looked at her as though her entire speech surprised him. "What do you do?"

She liked surprising him. She threw him a sassy grin. "I sling hash."

The look of shock on his face astonished her, though she had to admit that the thought of working in a greasy spoon would once have sent her reeling as well. And if her mother ever found out, she would probably have her committed to a home for dangerously unbalanced young ladies.

"Actually, it's in a very nice little restaurant in town. We serve Pacific Rim fusion food, things like mu shu pork in tortillas and Cornish game hens in Thai peanut sauce."

He was still staring at her as though he didn't believe a word she said. She waited for a moment, then shrugged, feeling a little wobbly herself.

"It's not all that extraordinary," she said with a touch of irritation. "What did you think I was, a lady of leisure or something?"

"No, I sure didn't think that," he said quickly. Then he frowned, seeing something behind her. "Is that your kid?" he asked.

She turned and saw Robbie at the door. The moment her gaze caught him, he slipped back into the house, and she shaded her eyes, wondering why he was acting uncharacteristically shy. "Yes, that's him," she said, then she gestured toward the house. "Come on," she told him seriously. "Let's get you fed and rested and then I'll figure out where I'm going to put you for the night."

That brought a quick reaction from him. Something deep in his eyes changed and he straightened, rubbing his chin with the heel of his hand. "No, listen, I'm out of here. I was just trying to split a few of your logs to try to pay you back for all you've done. I've got to get going, get up to my cabin and..."

His mind on his excuses, he made the mistake of trying to take a step toward her by putting weight on his weak leg and it deserted him entirely. He lurched and she sprang forward to break his fall. Her body caught his and her hand grasped the hard curve of his biceps, and the immediate sense of coming in contact with a man went through her as though she'd been struck by lightning.

"Here, lean on me," she managed to get out around the catch in her breath. She knew she was quivering with a visceral reaction to his physical strength, she only hoped he didn't notice. His body was long and hard and her own body was responding to it in a way she hadn't felt for years—a way she hadn't expected—a way that made her want to stop and listen to her heart beating like a captured thing in her chest.

Dangerous. The word echoed in her mind. He was danger all right, but that didn't mean she had to give in to it.

"I don't think so," he was saying, pulling away from her so quickly, it was almost a recoil. "I don't need help. I've got to do this on my own."

He started toward the house and she followed slowly, trying to calm herself. This was wild. She never did things like this. But her body seemed to have a will of its own today. And she had to admit—it was pretty exhilarating.

"I'll get out of your way," he muttered, starting to bypass the house.

"No," she cried, jumping forward and slipping her hand into the crook of his arm. "You come on in the house. I'm going to feed you, at least. Look at you, practically wasting away here."

He turned his head and met her gaze and she felt as though he saw right through her, knew she'd grabbed his arm because she wanted to feel his muscles again, knew she wanted to keep him around as long as she could—just because. A flush filled her cheeks, but she didn't care. That sparkling feeling was filling her with a sense of life she hadn't had in a long time.

"Come on," she urged, tugging on his arm. "Come eat."

He came with her, but reluctantly, and he let her lead him. She knew he hated feeling weak this way, but she also had a feeling that wasn't all there was to his hesitation. The awareness that had sparked between them earlier had come to life again when she'd broken his fall and held him for a split second, and she could tell that he felt it too, and that he wasn't happy about it. Turning resolutely, she led the way to the house, chattering about the weather.

"Sit down," she told him as they entered the dining room. "I'll have the food on the table in no time."

Denver hesitated as though he were about to argue, but the aroma of pot roast simmering wafted in from the kitchen and his resistance seemed to melt away. He lowered himself carefully to a seat at the table and she pretended not to be watching him out of the corner of her eye to make sure he made it. Turning, she glanced around the room. Robbie was nowhere to be seen and she set off to find out why.

She found him in his bedroom and took him to the bathroom to wash his hands. He came willingly enough, but he seemed worried about something.

"Mom. Who is that man?" he asked her as he soaped up, his eyes wary.

"He's my friend," she told him, turning off the water to hurry him along. "Do you want to come and meet him?"

Robbie frowned, taking his time, washing his hands as though it were a heavy responsibility. "Is he the surprise?" he asked, then shot a quick glance at her face.

She smiled as she turned the faucet back on for a rinse. "Yes. He's the surprise. I thought you'd like having a man come to dinner. We don't have men around here very often, do we?"

Robbie shook his head, thinking that over. "He's awful big," he said at last.

Charlie laughed. "Yes, he is, isn't he?"

His freckled nose wrinkled. "Are you sure he likes boys?" he asked her.

"Of course." She answered without thinking, handing him a towel. "Doesn't everybody?"

He shook his head vehemently. "No. Mrs. Rathworth doesn't. She always yells when I go by her house. She tells me to stay away from her yard."

Charlie became serious suddenly, her head to the side as she gazed at him. "Have you ever gone in her yard?" she asked.

He shook his head. "But some of the fifth-graders did," he told her as though in confidence. "They picked a bunch of her apples right off her tree."

"Well, there. You see? There's usually a reason when someone seems too mean. It's usually because someone has been mean to them. You have to think about that before you get mad."

"Okay," he said agreeably. "Look." He held up his hands for inspection. "All clean."

"Clean as a whistle," she agreed, and they left the bathroom behind.

She led him out into the dining area and introduced him to Denver, who nodded to the boy but seemed to look right through him. Robbie followed her into the kitchen rather than stay at the table with him, and she took advantage of his presence and loaded him up with things to carry back out for the dining table. With help from the microwave, she had everything steaming hot in minutes, and soon they were passing serving dishes and getting ready to eat. Charlie looked over the scene and smiled. Something felt good about it.

"Cheers," she said, raising her glass of milk to toast the other two.

Neither of them said a word, and they raised their glasses reluctantly, but she didn't let it spoil her mood. She basked in the glow. This was as close to a family meal as this place had ever had.

And darn it all, this was good.

Four

The pot roast was out of this world. Denver had to restrain himself from closing his eyes as he savored every morsel.

"This meat is great," he told Charlie, though he did so awkwardly. He wasn't one who was used to complimenting the chef. "Too bad all mothers don't teach their daughters to cook like this."

She laughed. "My mother has never cooked a pot roast in her life," she said happily, wanting to break into giggles at the thought of her formal, dignified mother in an apron with flour on her nose. "She's probably not even sure what kind of meat you use." She put a piece of that very same meat on her fork and regarded it kindly. "But she can plan a menu for three hundred at a charity luncheon, which is something I'll never know how to do," she added softly, then flushed, wishing she hadn't said it. People must think it strange to hear her say a thing like that. She glanced at Denver to see what he was thinking.

Denver swallowed another delicious bite and avoided her gaze, wondering how he'd forgotten. Of course, he knew all about her mother and what kind of people she came from. Charlie seemed so different now, it was hard to keep that in mind.

He glanced down the table and looked at her. She was saying something to her son and it gave him a chance to study her without being noticed. She was pretty and quick-witted and her eyes shone with amusement most of the time. Had she always been this way? Not in his memory. He remembered how she'd looked the last time he saw her, years ago.

It was graduation day at the Arcadana Academy. He'd gone to watch his sister, Gail, walk up on the stage and receive her diploma. He'd been bursting with pride. She'd looked just like the others, tall and slim and beautiful, full of laughter, graceful as a bird. You couldn't tell she was any different, he'd told himself. You couldn't see that her father had swung a pickax for a living, that her parents hadn't been made of money, with generations of breeding and privilege behind them, like the others. Gail looked as though she belonged. That was what he'd dreamed of for her, what he'd worked his tail off to provide for her. And now it had all seemed worthwhile.

He'd hung back after the ceremony, watching her being introduced to the families and friends of other girls. He didn't want to embarrass her. There was no way anyone would ever confuse him with a blue blood, a fact that didn't usually bother him. His broad shoulders hadn't been earned by hours on the tennis court, and his tan was a product of the Sahara Desert, not the country club golf course. His hair was a little too long and his clothes looked a little too rumpled. Though he traveled a lot, his style was too plebeian for the jet-setters, and he had no interest in that sort of thing. But he didn't want to cramp his sister's style. It made him happy to see her succeed, to see her fit in.

Suddenly, she saw him and her face changed. With a shriek, she ran to meet him, throwing her arms around his neck, not caring who saw her embrace her rough brother. His heart had filled with love for her, but as he looked back to where she'd run from, he saw the others watching. Charlyne—as she'd been called then—was pointing at Gail and laughing, turning to say something to one of the others, and Denver reddened and pushed Gail away, sure the beautiful but obviously spoiled young woman was making fun of Gail's brother.

"I just came to see you graduate," he'd told her gruffly, purposely turning away from Charlyne. "I've got to get going."

His sister had seemed to regret that, her huge eyes filling with sorrow. "Oh, but, Denver, we're having a dinner at the Chez Sateau. You must come."

His grin was slightly crooked. She even knew how to talk like the others. He shook his head.

"Can't. Got an assignment and I'm due at the airport. I'll see you later in the week, at home. You go on back to your friends."

He'd looked at Charlyne as Gail walked away. She was looking right back at him, but now she wasn't laughing. Their gazes met and held for a moment. Denver had hoped she couldn't see how much he resented her. He pulled his gaze away, turned on his heel, and left for the parking lot.

Now he looked at the woman who had once called herself Charlyne. Her body was fuller, softer-looking, and her angular face had filled in with lovely curves. Where he'd once seen snobbery there was nothing but warmth. It hardly seemed possible that this Charlie was the same woman. He wished he knew what had brought on such a change in the weather.

But he frowned as he savored his last bite of meat. Years of undercover work had developed a strong streak of cynicism in him. People didn't change that much. Maybe she'd just learned to hide what she really was. Maybe that was all there was to it.

He let the current scene come back into his senses again. Charlie was talking seriously to her son, telling him that no, he was not going to get a rifle until he was much, much older.

"Billy has one."

"Billy can have a hundred. That is not going to make a difference to us. You're too young. And guns are disgusting anyway."

The boy looked at Denver as if he were waiting for him to jump in here, but Denver didn't have an opinion one way or the other, and Robbie looked away again, disappointed. Denver felt his disappointment and shrugged. There was nothing he could do here. He'd had a rifle by the time he was six himself, but his family had lived in the country. Things were different in those days. He couldn't imagine giving this infant child a rifle to carry around with him. Charlie was right. The kid didn't need it.

He had to laugh at the irony, though. Here he was, a man who lived a life where a gun was an absolute necessity, and he didn't want to see the boy use one. Maybe he was losing his edge. Maybe it was time to start thinking about a life after the dangerous one he'd been leading all these years. "You can't do this forever," a friend had said to him only a few days ago. "Go out and find yourself a woman and have a family." He'd laughed at the time. The thought had been ludicrous. But somehow it didn't seem quite so funny right now.

Looking across the table, he found the boy staring at him as though he were a specimen that might need dissecting. Before he could look away again, the child spoke to him for the first time.

"Hey, mister," he said softly, looking a little shy but determined. "Did you ever catch a three-pound golden trout?"

Denver blinked. It seemed an odd question. But then, kids were odd. He never had got the hang of dealing with them. "Can't say that I have," he answered gruffly, hoping that would satisfy him.

The boy's stare grew more intense. "Billy's dad did," he said, as though that proved something.

Denver wanted to ask who the hell Billy was, but he stopped himself in time, and luckily, Charlie caught his attention.

"More?" she was asking.

He shook his head. "It was great," he told her, and it was true, but he was definitely full. He couldn't remember when a woman had last cooked for him like this. Looking at her, he wished he could tell her how much it meant to him. But on second thought, maybe it would be better to let it go.

She cleared away a few dishes, then settled back in

her chair and smiled at him as though ready for the next item on her agenda, and he tensed, ready to run.

"So, Mr. Denver Smith," she said pleasantly. "How long are you planning to stay?"

"About five more minutes," he drawled, avoiding her gaze.

"No," she responded with a quick laugh. "I mean here at the lake."

"A few weeks," he said, not filling in any details. After-dinner chitchat had never been one of his favorite activities.

"What made you come here to our little two-horse town?" she asked, glancing around the table to see if anyone needed anything. "All we've got is the lake and a broken-down ski lift Hal Waters is trying to sell to some gullible flatlander. We don't get too many…" She stopped and pretended to blot at a spill with her napkin. She was going to say "men like you" but then she realized that might be a little too blatant a compliment. "Anyway, what made you come here?"

He shrugged. "I wasn't looking for a tourist trap. I'm not staying long."

"And then what will you be going back to?" she asked.

He glanced at her, amused. He knew what she was up to, and he knew she knew he knew. But that didn't mean she was going to get what she was after. "I suppose I'll be going back to where I came from," he told her casually.

She blinked, then leaned forward, her jaw at a determined angle, reminding him suddenly of her child. "And where, exactly, is that?" she insisted, her deep violet eyes pinning him to the wall.

He put off answering long enough to see those eyes

flare with indignation before he gave her a tidbit. "I've got an apartment," he admitted at last, suddenly feeling a little silly about being so close-mouthed. Years of training had made him that way. Experience and natural suspicion had intensified the instinct to keep his private life private—even from friends. But it could be he was going a little far here. After all, what would it hurt to tell Charlie a few things about himself? "I'm not there much, but it's sort of a home base. It's in San Francisco."

"San Francisco." She nodded, and there was a far-away look in her eyes. "I was born there."

"Really?" Turn about was fair play, wasn't it? "What brought you out here to the mountains instead?"

Her smile was brief and noncommittal. "I like the mountains," she said evasively, rising and reaching for his plate. "There's dessert, and I won't hear 'no' from you. You just sit tight for another minute or two."

Obediently, he stayed where he was, but he knew she was being as elusive as he was. That was odd, and yet it fit in with everything else she'd said today. She was here under an assumed name and she wanted to leave her past out of it. What was she running from? It would be very interesting to find out. And what would she do if she knew he recognized her? He hadn't planned to tell her at all, assuming he wouldn't be around long enough for it to matter. But now that he'd lingered this long, it hardly seemed fair to keep her in the dark. He ought to say something. Maybe he would.

There was a noise from the end of the table and suddenly he realized he was alone with the kid again.

He knew he should make an effort to talk to him. He glanced at him, disconcerted to find the blue-eyed stare still glued to his own face. What was with the kid, anyway? He stirred uncomfortably and tried to think of something to say that a boy this age might be interested in.

"So, how do you like school?" he asked lamely.

The boy merely stared harder, and Denver gave a mental shrug. Oh, well. He'd tried. There wasn't much point to conversation with Robbie anyway. He was probably a punk. Most of the kids he'd known lately had been punks. Admittedly, they were a bit older than this one. Robbie still had baby fat and the round eyes of an innocent. But the potential for punkhood was always there.

Still, he probably ought to try again.

"Do you like to play ball?" he asked. "Soccer? Don't all kids play soccer these days?"

Robbie shook his head. "I like to swim," he offered hopefully.

"Swim, huh?" The last time he'd been swimming it had been in a South American rain forest and he'd had to pry the leeches off afterwards. "I'm not a big swimming fan." He stared into his glass and tried not to remember the leeches.

When he looked up again, he could see that the boy had a look of disappointment on his face. Denver wasn't sure why, but he was pretty certain it had something to do with him. Before he could analyze the situation fully, the boy put another question to him.

"Do you have any kids?" he asked.

Denver shook his head. "Nope. Not me."

Robbie hesitated, then asked tentatively, "Not even a secret kid?" His eyes were hooded, but intent.

Denver stared at him, startled. What did a child this age know about things like that? "Not that I know of," he said shortly, feeling as though he'd been accused of something. "No, I'm sure of it. I don't have a kid."

Robbie blinked and his lower lip quivered for a moment. But that passed quickly and his young face took on a look of defiance and his little chin rose. "Did you ever fly a jet plane?" he asked, his blue-eyed stare as hard as the light during an old-fashioned interrogator's third degree.

Denver shook his head. "Nope."

The boy's lips tipped into a tiny hint of a smile. "Billy's dad did."

Denver felt a muscle near his temple twitch. "No kidding," he said. Billy again. It was clear from the look on Robbie's face that he thought Billy was a lucky boy. Fortunately, the subject was quickly overshadowed by the arrival of Charlie with the dessert.

"Cherry pie," she announced, and Denver groaned. Cherry pie was his favorite. No matter how full he was, he always had room for cherry pie.

But as he waited in anticipation, he was aware that the boy had leaned across the table and was trying to catch his eye. Reluctantly, he faced him.

"Did you ever wrestle a gorilla?" the boy asked, eyes bright and earnest.

Denver stared at him for a split second, then twitched with annoyance. "I know, I know, Billy's dad did."

Robbie nodded solemnly, not letting up a bit. "Uh-huh."

Denver restrained the snarling instinct that rose to

fill him. "Billy's dad must be quite a man," he said instead, his tone even.

Robbie nodded again. "He is."

Denver glanced at Charlie, who was intent upon cutting the pie, her bottom lip caught behind her teeth as she concentrated. He turned back to the kid. There had to be something he could say to put this boy back on his heels. After all, who was the adult here?

"So Billy's dad told you he did all these things, did he?" he asked, with one eyebrow raised.

Robbie's face was clear as a choir boy's. "No. *He* didn't tell me." He stared into Denver's gaze. "Billy's dad doesn't ever brag."

Denver winced as though he'd taken a mortal blow. If Charlie hadn't been right there, he might just have resorted to swearing. He felt like a man who'd lost a fight to some guy who hadn't even showed up.

"Of course," he said softly. "What was I thinking?"

Robbie nodded, obviously happy that the pecking order had been firmly established. "Billy tells me all about it," he offered serenely.

Denver stared down at the piece of cherry pie Charlie had passed him. He'd just been wiped out by a five-year-old, and he knew it. Slowly, he began to realize just how funny that was. Looking up, he caught Robbie's eye and he began to grin. Caught off guard, the boy almost grinned back. It might have been a defining moment if the telephone hadn't rung at exactly that point, and in a shot, Robbie was off the chair and running for it.

"You didn't ask to be excused," Charlie called after him, shaking her head as he ignored her and grabbed the receiver. "That will be his friend Billy," she told Denver in explanation. "Since there's no school tomorrow, Billy's family has invited him to go along into Blackthorne to pizza and a movie. He has a great time with Billy."

"And Billy's superhero dad," Denver murmured, taking another bite of pie. "Got any idea where I can get hold of some kryptonite?"

She'd been half listening to her son's progress as he got off the phone and began to get ready to go, but she turned back to ask Denver, "What's that?"

He shook his head. "Nothing," he said softly, finishing his pie. In the distance, he could hear Robbie calling questions to her, and Charlie answering, but he wasn't paying attention to what was being said.

Something had shifted, a ray of light or an angle or something, and he was really seeing her again, seeing her as she looked against the background of the forest through the window, seeing her lovely face and her huge, soft eyes and feeling something twist inside him, and he knew this was a trap. She might not mean it that way, but facts were facts. If he let himself, he could end up caught in a web that might scar him for life in a way his physical injuries never had been able to do.

Okay, it was time to get out of here. He wasn't sure how he was going to make it up that steep hill, but he was going to do it. Taking a deep breath, he pulled himself to his feet, apologized for not being in the proper condition to help her clean up, and started for the door.

"Hey, hold on there," she called after him.

He stopped, his back still to her. "Look, Charlie, I've got to get back to my cabin," he began, determined to be tough with her.

But she was rushing her son past him to the door because there was someone honking outside, and she was not even listening to him.

"Bye," she called, waving as the car backed out of the driveway. Denver came up behind her and watched the headlights sweep the trees. The car was gone in seconds and they were all alone.

"Thanks for that great meal," he said gruffly, glancing at her sideways and preparing to take off very quickly. "I think it was just what I needed to give me the strength to…"

She turned and took one look at him and shook her head. "Oh, no, you don't. You're not climbing that hill on your own," she told him firmly, the light of her own determination in her eyes.

His temple twitched. "I don't know how else I'm getting there," he said. "You can obviously take care of a lot of things, Charlie, but you can't carry me on your back."

"No, I can't do that." Her grin was annoyingly impish as she swept back her hair and looked him full in the face. "But I can sure as heck carry you on my scooter."

"Scooter?" he echoed doubtfully, and for one insane moment, a picture of her pushing along on the child's toy flashed through his head, but he knew she must mean a motor scooter.

"It's a great little vehicle," she assured him. "I'll pop you on the back, and off we'll go."

There was no way. He couldn't even imagine it. His brows knit together in consternation as he looked down at her. "There's no road going up there."

"There's a path. That's good enough. You wait right here."

"No, Charlie…"

She didn't wait to hear what he had to say, and the smile she wore as she disappeared around the corner of the house was just this side of sassy. He growled and began to walk as normally as he was able down the steps and off her porch. There was no way he was riding on a mosquito-sized motor scooter up that rough hill.

There was no way. *No way.*

Actually, the little bike had a lot of pep for its size, considering it was carrying two people on its back. She drove it like a racer, leaning into the curves, and he probably would have gotten a kick out of the look of sheer tenacity on her face as she forced it uphill, but he was too busy trying not to hold her too tightly or touch her in forbidden places.

It was hard enough holding on with his bad leg stretched out and the rocks making regular appearances underneath the wheels. Not only did he have to worry about flying off the thing, he also had to worry about the fact that Charlie's silky hair was wrapping itself around his face, sending her deliciously spicy scent right into his brain, working to numb his inhibitions and do in his conscience. And at the same time, his hands, which he'd perched impersonally at her waist after he'd failed to find anything else to hang on to other than the tattered shreds tearing away at the back of the seat—those same hands were slipping down to take hold of her hip bones, his fingers curling into her soft belly, conjuring up images of misty nights on satin sheets. To add insult to injury, when she bent back a certain way, he could see right down her shirt, see the lovely round breasts that disappeared only vaguely into an almost transparent lacy bra and he could even catch a hint of the darkening at the tips if she bent far enough. And, much as he hated himself, he couldn't avert his gaze and avoid the scene. He tried closing his eyes, but that was worse. He tried concentrating on the pain in his knee, but it seemed to be gone.

Hey, maybe he'd discovered something. Libido as a pain killer. He should write it up and submit it to some medical journal. But not now. Right now he had to concentrate on how good she smelled and how soft she felt and...

"Jerk," he muttered to himself, fighting hard to ignore his senses, which were all going into overload at once.

"What?" she called back, her hair slapping his face in a way that made torture seem like fun.

"Nothing," he returned gruffly, pretending to hate all that he was going through, when in all actuality, his soul was melting into a puddle of desire at her lovely feet.

"There it is," she told him, revving the motor in an encouraging way. "We're almost there."

"Good," he said under his breath. Much more of this and he would be writhing in exquisite agony by the time they landed in a spot where he could go off and hide.

But just when they had almost made it, the little engine seemed to lose heart. It sputtered and groaned and he held his breath, willing the machine to keep on trying.

"Don't worry," she shouted over the sound of the motor as it caught again. "This is the little scooter that could."

"Cute," he said, but he got her hair in his mouth and it tasted like cotton candy.

Finally they arrived and she helped him off the scooter, even as he tried to resist accepting any assistance at all. Turning, she shaded her eyes against the last rays of the sun as it slid behind the mountains, and looked at the cabin.

"Say, this is the old McHenry place, isn't it?"

He started toward the porch, limping but not really in much pain. "Who is old McHenry?" he asked.

Laughter seemed to bubble up from her for the slightest of reasons, and it happened again now. "*He* wasn't old, and his name was Carlos McHenry."

"Carlos?"

"Mm-hmm." She started to follow him up the steps. "His mother was Spanish or something. No one's lived here for years, not since he did. I wonder why they gave it to you?"

"I said I wanted someplace really remote when I called the reservation service."

"This is remote, all right." She gazed up at the cobwebs in the porch rafters and made a face. "They say that was why Carlos McHenry liked it, too." They were facing each other as he pulled out his key and she gave him a significant look. "Legend has it that he did some pretty weird stuff up here in those days."

The dull ache that had started on the motor scooter was still hanging on in his gut. It made him restless and gruff, but he held his feelings at bay and tried to be polite. "Oh yeah?" he replied to her comment. "What kind of weird stuff? Bodies in the basement?"

She shrugged. "More like lovers in the laundry basket."

"Ouch. Sounds uncomfortable."

She giggled. "Maybe they were very small."

He gazed down at her. The tousled hair was floating around her face and her eyes were sparkling provocatively. It was a face a man could fall in love with.

But not him. Things like love were for others, not for him. Falling in love had always seemed like a sign of weakness to him, and the last thing he wanted to show anyone was weakness.

"Do you just say anything that pops into your head?" he asked her as he turned the key in the lock, forcing a return to an irritable grumpiness he really didn't feel anymore. A man had to do something to keep a beautiful woman at bay. *Think Humphrey Bogart,* he told himself silently. But somehow Cary Grant kept getting in the way.

She shrugged at his words, as though the thought that she might be talking silliness had never occurred to her before. She followed him in as he made his way into the darkened room, gazing about curiously as he lit the lantern hanging over the table.

"No electricity?" she asked, but didn't wait for an answer, as that was pretty obvious. "This place is really spooky. Are you sure you want to stay here?"

He followed her gaze and saw what she was seeing. The couch was broken down, the coffee table an old tree stump. The painting hanging on the wall was of riders roughing it through purple sage and looked as though it had been a thrift-shop item even back in the forties. The floor creaked and the rug had spots worn almost through to the wood. The place had none of the warm, inviting elements that graced her own home. But this was much more his style, much more what he was used to.

"I like it," he told her, then looked pointedly at the

door. It would be best to get her out of here before
things got any dicier. "Thanks for everything, Charlie.
I really appreciate all you've done."

"It was nothing," she told him impudently. "I
would have done the same for a wolf caught in a
trap." She grinned at him as she passed, still looking
over the room and evidently not ready to take the hint
about leaving. "And he would probably have been just
as cranky as you are," she noted, turning to look at
the sad old painting.

"At least I don't bite," he murmured, watching her.

She turned her head and gave him a long, sideways
glance. "Don't you?" she asked softly.

It came over him like a wave, the overwhelming
need to pull her into his arms and try out her neck.
His hands knotted into fists and he tensed, fighting
back all his instincts. He had to get her out of here
before he did something deliciously stupid, something
he would relish for the moment and then have to regret
for the rest of his life.

"You'd better go," he told her abruptly. "I'm
pretty tired. I'd like to get some rest."

She turned, suddenly all concern for his well-being.
"Are you sure you're okay?" she asked, starting toward him. "Your leg is still bad. Denver, I really wish
you'd see a doctor. Can I help you?…"

"Just go." He stepped back before she could touch
him. "I'm fine. I can take care of myself."

She sighed, dropping her hand to her side. "I hate
to leave you like this," she said. "But I guess I will
go. I really have to get back. I'm late for work."

He was leaning against a chair and he wanted to sit
down, but he was damned if he'd let her see him give

way to that. "Go on, get out of here. I don't need a nursemaid."

She hesitated. "But your knee…"

He frowned at her, exasperated. "Look, I've been through a lot worse things in my time. I once had to dig a bullet out of my own thigh with a Swiss army knife. This is a piece of cake compared to that. I can handle it."

Her eyes widened with shock and then winced with the horror of it. "You dug a bullet out of your thigh? Where were you? What were you doing?"

"Removing a bullet. I thought I mentioned that." He shook his head, forestalling her response. "It's a long story. The details are too boring to bring up now. But the bottom line is, situations arrive and you deal with them."

But her face had changed. Pure skepticism now glinted from her huge violet eyes. She had the look of a mother whose kid had just claimed an elephant had come in when she wasn't looking and knocked over his cup of milk. "You're making it up, aren't you? Just to throw me off."

He looked at her and saw the girl at graduation, all superior and mocking and he was glad to see that old supercilious Charlyne back again. She was easier to deal with. She was easier to dislike.

"Fine, if that makes you feel better," he said evenly. "The point is, I'm okay. Go."

She licked her lower lip, frowning. "Are you sure.…"

He reached out and pulled the door all the way open, gesturing for her to use it. "I don't need you, okay?" he told her firmly. *Sometimes you have to be cruel to be kind,* he told himself silently. "I can take care of myself. You're only in the way. I don't want anything from you."

"You don't need me, huh?" she repeated softly, then lifted her chin. "Then give me back that pot roast. *And* the cherry pie."

For the first time in his life, he knew what it felt like to want to roll his eyes. "Get out of here," he said instead, exasperation unmistakable.

They stared at each other for a long moment, and he held his breath. If she took a step toward him...if she touched him...he wasn't sure he would be able to keep from doing what every impulse in him was urging. But she broke the spell first, turning from him.

"I'm going, I'm going," she said lightly, taking it as though he were teasing. She went out through the front door, glanced back and gave him a little wave. He closed the door firmly and she couldn't help but smile.

"But I'll be coming back," she muttered under her breath as she turned back toward her scooter. "You can't get rid of me that easily, Mr. Smith."

Five

Charlie was late for work, but the owners always treated her just like family and as she pulled up beside the little restaurant on her scooter, trying to explain before she even got off the thing, her boss, Ernie, waved away her excuses just as he always did.

"I know you ladies all have things to do," he said good-naturedly. "Or you start to talk and the time just goes on, leaving you behind. You don't have to tell me about it. I've got a wife, don't I?"

Charlie gave him a mock look of outrage and called him a male chauvinist, but he only laughed and shrugged away her protests. They had a nice easy-going rapport that had helped her through more than one crisis in the past few years.

"Where's my boy?" Ernie asked, looking behind her for her son, who was usually with her and usually ready to give Ernie a big bear hug, complete with growling noises. "Did you lose him?"

Charlie laughed, shaking her head. Ernie was a large man, part Hawaiian, part just about everything else you could name, and all good nature. He laughed a lot and cried at sad stories and sang old hula ballads with ukulele accompaniment when he'd had too much to drink. He and his wife were her best friends here in the valley.

She often remembered when she'd first come into the café, cold and broke and pregnant, not sure where she was going or how long she could go on, counting out her pennies to see if she had enough to buy a hamburger, and Ernie had come up from behind and taken in the situation at a glance.

"So, what you want?" he'd asked her, leaning over her with a jovial smile.

She'd just come in out of the rain and she pushed back her stringy, soggy hair and tried to focus on the man. "Uh...maybe a tuna sandwich..." she'd said, trying to catch a dime that was about to roll off the table.

"Nah." He shook his headful of beautiful black hair. "I saw you lookin' at the burger. You look to me like you need something to stick to your ribs. Burger and fries, comin' up."

She'd blinked at him, unsure how to react to this sort of thing. "But I don't have enough...."

"Forget the money." He moved quickly, pushing her coins back off the table and into her purse. "I'm tryin' out a new recipe. I need a tester. You can help me."

He'd brought her a huge burger, along with fries and coleslaw and sliced fruit and a tall glass of milk that seemed to be refilled every time she turned her attention away, and then he'd brought out Michiko, the tiny, very pretty woman who was his wife, and introduced the two of them. From that moment on, Charlie had people who cared about her, people she could rely on in a pinch. She'd started working for them the next day, sleeping on their couch until she'd saved enough to start paying rent on the cabin. They'd held her hand when she'd delivered Robbie and they'd let her bring him in to work with her from the first.

"Let her" was putting it mildly, she thought now, her affection for these two friends bringing tears to her eyes. They'd demanded Robbie come along. They'd spent almost as much time oohing and aahing over him as she had. It had been her lucky day when she'd stumbled into the Pali and made these two friends.

"Robbie's not with me tonight," she told Ernie now. "He's going for pizza and a movie with the Howells. He's even going to stay all night, so he was pretty excited."

"What about school?" Ernie asked, always looking out for Robbie's welfare.

"No school tomorrow. Teachers' conference day or something like that." She looked at him and said, almost in wonder, "So I'm on my own for once."

"Hey, now's your chance," Ernie teased her. "Get yourself a hot date with that guy who's been hanging around all month. He's been dying to take you out."

She gave him a horrified grimace. "You mean that Nigel person? The one who comes in and orders coffee and then sits there nursing it while he follows every move I make for the next two hours?" She shuddered. "I think not, Ernie. I've been married, you know. I learned my lesson.'' She threw him a sassy grin. "A good book is better than a man any day.''

She turned to go on into the café and Ernie called after her, "A good book may be better than a *bad* man, honey, but when the right *good* guy comes along, you're going to fall like water over the dam.''

"Yeah,'' she quipped over her shoulder. "But I'll be falling into a hiding place, not into his arms. You can bet on that one.''

He laughed and as she went inside, the feeling of well-being was growing in her. And now she knew it had very little to do with Denver Smith, because that was over, really. It had been fun to have him in her house, fun to make a meal for a man.

And—come on, she might as well admit it. It had been fun to have an attractive man look at her with hungry eyes. She had never been a tease, but she knew when a man wanted her. It was probably lucky for both of them that he'd had the sense to leash that desire and not try to take advantage of the situation. You had to respect a man who was willing to do that. Too bad there weren't more of them in this world.

But as far as she was concerned, Denver had been a one-day wonder, and that was that. She'd built a life here in the mountains, a life she loved. She'd created a protected circle to raise Robbie inside of, a magic, peaceful place that wouldn't take well to having a man around, crashing against the sides and wanting to change things. She had to maintain those walls or things might get out of hand again, and everything she'd worked so hard for would be ruined.

She was quite serious in her aversion to getting entangled with a man. She'd been entangled with Jeff van Grote and that had taught her all she wanted to know about men. Falling in love—well, falling in love with the idea of being in love was probably more like it—anyway, it had been fun and the wedding had been lovely.

But the wedding night had been an unpleasant chore more than anything else. She'd finally had herself a lover and she'd found out the truth. Romantic stories had it all wrong. Men were the ones who enjoyed that sort of thing. Women were just there to make it possible for them.

No, she'd had about as much fun as she could allow herself with a man with Denver that evening. There really shouldn't be any return engagement, even though she'd been tempted to think so as she left him. She had more important things to do—like raise her son. She had a life to live.

In the café, she saw that Michiko was serving a young couple at the window table and she waved. The place was almost empty. It was going to be a slow night.

She put on an apron and began filling salt cellars, and Michiko came bustling past her, heading for the kitchen. "Two bowls of saimin," she said as she passed. "Can you get it, please?" She shook her head and glanced out the window at the gathering gloom. "You can tell there's a chill in the air today. Everyone wants saimin."

Charlie laughed and nodded. "It does help that you've got it simmering—so the first thing anyone smells when they step inside is that heavenly aroma," she noted, spooning up a bowl of the delicious noodle soup with the tiny pieces of red barbecued pork floating on the surface.

"Aha!" Michiko cried, laughing. "You guessed my secret weapon!"

Charlie served the young couple, talking to them in the casual fashion they all had fallen into here at the Pali, as though everyone was familiar, everyone was a local, everyone was bound to be a friend. She was smiling as she turned back, feeling satisfied with her life, looking at the shiny tablecloths on the rustic tables glowing yellow under the flickering light of each candle and feeling a welling up of peace and contentment.

"I am so glad I ran," she murmured to herself as she began wiping down the counter. "I am so glad I came here."

A new customer came in through the swinging door. Charlie looked up and waved a greeting at Goldie, an eccentric older woman who lived high in the mountains and came down to the valley for her supplies two or three times a year.

"Is it that time again already?" Charlie said lightly, showing Goldie to her favorite booth.

The woman only came up to Charlie's shoulder, which she patted as she took her seat, shaking her head of gray hair, which she carefully coiled in a long braid around the crown of her head. "No, this was a special trip. I've been out of town and I'm heading for home. But you know very well I can't go through without having my bowl of Michiko's saimin soup."

"Of course not. I'll bring you some right away."

Goldie always touched something in Charlie, brought out her mothering instincts. She'd often worried about the woman in the past, wondering how such a seemingly vulnerable person could live such a rough and isolated life.

"Broken heart," Michiko had told her when she'd asked about it, nodding her head with sympathy. "That's what always does it. Her husband left her years ago and she ran away into the mountains to hide from the pain."

Charlie could understand that to some degree. "What does she do up there all alone?" she'd asked Michiko the first time she'd served a bowl of soup to Goldie.

"Oh, she's one of those science ladies. You know, like Jane Goodall and the chimpanzees? She studies animals."

"What kind of animals?"

"I don't know, I think some sort of squirrels or rats or something like that." She'd shrugged. "Someday she'll write a book or do a show on it or something and we'll know somebody famous. Just you wait and see."

They'd all been waiting, but they still hadn't seen fame and fortune come Goldie's way, and Charlie had a feeling they never would. Still, the woman seemed happy enough, and she supposed that was what counted in the end.

She set the bowl of soup in front of her and nodded toward the suitcase sitting beside Goldie's chair. "Was it a long trip?"

"Just to San Diego. I went to see my son about some business. Some papers I had to have signed."

Charlie's eyes widened. "You have a son? I've never seen him. I didn't know...."

"Oh yes. In fact, he was just about the age of your boy when he and I moved here. We rented that old cabin out by the crossroads while he was young. This is such a good place to raise a boy, isn't it?"

Charlie nodded, pleased to find they had this in common. In her mind, Goldie's son looked like Robbie, all grown up. "Oh, I agree. I'll bet your boy turned out great. I'd love to meet him. When was the last time he came to visit?"

Goldie's face changed and she looked down, her fingers twisting nervously in her napkin as she spread it on her lap. "Oh, he doesn't have time for that," she said quickly. "No, he's much too busy. He's director of a very large organization and he is always going on business trips. He and his wife are always entertaining...." Her voice trailed off and Charlie looked away, embarrassed for her.

They chatted a moment or two more while her soup cooled, and then Charlie went back to wrapping the tableware in napkins for place settings. But what Goldie had told her—and what she hadn't said—stuck with her. So the older woman had raised a boy alone in the mountains, just as she was doing. And now she was all alone, and her son never came to see her....

There was something so unutterably sad and depressing about that scenario, she didn't want to think about it. And yet, she couldn't get it out of her mind. Turning from the counter, she stopped to drop a quarter she'd found in the cash register, and that was when she saw it. Her own picture was staring at her from where it was propped next to the tip can.

Time stood still and she felt as though the walls had dropped away. She was standing on a precipice, all alone, out in the middle of nowhere. Time started moving again, but it was slow, oh so slow, and she ached to make it move faster, so that she could react, so that she could see what had happened and what to do about it.

But as things came back to speed, she reached out to steady herself, because the room seemed to have tilted. Then, she just stared at the picture, paralyzed to the tips of her toes, not moving a muscle. It was her all right, with her hair cut in that phony gamine style her mother loved, wearing a false smile and a pink cashmere sweater. Her high school yearbook photo. How…where…?

Acting purely on instinct, she reached out to hide it, to throw it away, do something with it. She wanted to erase it, make it not be there. But before her fingers had curled around it, Michiko spoke from behind her.

"Oh, you saw the picture," she said, nodding toward it as she hurried through toward the kitchen. "Some guy was in here earlier. He left it. Take a look. See what you think." And she disappeared through the swinging doors.

Charlie's mouth was full of cotton. She couldn't have said a word if she'd wanted to. Some guy…what guy? Some man had come in and left Michiko a picture of her…why? Who?

But she knew the answer without having to be told, and slowly she began to breathe normally again, staring at the picture and wishing she could ignite it with her gaze, set it on fire, make it disappear. It was a goofy-looking picture, but it was so definitely her. No one would be able to miss the resemblance. Now they knew. Now everyone would know. What was she going to do?

Michiko came back out, carrying menus for a new party that had arrived in the doorway. She paused, looking over Charlie's shoulder. "Cute, isn't she?" she said. "But she doesn't look very happy."

Charlie swallowed hard but she couldn't get words

to form. Neither could she look Michiko in the face, but her friend didn't seem to notice.

"The man was looking for her. He said the picture was about ten years old, so she might look a little different. What do you think?"

Michiko cocked her head to the side and studied it, and Charlie waited, hardly breathing, for her to notice. How could her friend miss it? It was right there, in front of her nose. The eyes might look sad, but they were Charlie's eyes. Couldn't she see it?

"I told him it wasn't anyone I knew," Michiko went on, talking over her shoulder as she left the room, "but he left it just in case anyone has seen her. There's a number to call." The door thumped behind her.

"Well, what do you know," Charlie whispered to herself in wonder. Michiko hadn't recognized her. She was still half safe. She swallowed, shook herself, and went back to work, but her mind was racing. This wasn't the first time someone looking for her had come close. There'd been a report on television when she'd first arrived, but no one in the area had really seen her yet except Michiko and Ernie, and they hadn't seemed to notice. A year or so later, after Robbie was born, she'd gone into Sacramento on a shopping trip with Michiko and she'd seen her own picture up on a market billboard. She'd gone to a telephone and called her mother's number that time, but Griggs, the butler, had answered saying her mother was at a meeting of some sort, and she'd left a message. "I'm okay, Mother," she'd told him to tell her. "Stop looking for me. I'm doing fine."

She'd run on an impulse, without the sort of planning that would usually make an escape like that a success. She'd packed a few things in a small bag, hidden her hair with a scarf, then taken the train, a bus, and a ride with a trucker, who'd dropped her here in the valley. She hadn't really thought her headlong run would succeed. She'd just done what she felt she had to do. And then she'd found this place and decided to stay until they found her.

But they hadn't found her, and little by little, this life had become normal to her. Now it seemed maybe she was in danger of losing it again, unless she could think of something, fast.

Okay. Her mother had hired someone to find her. That person had arrived in town and was passing her picture around. Michiko hadn't put the pieces together, but someone else probably would. She had only one choice. She had to go hide somewhere until things died down again. But this was different from when she'd run before. Then, she'd carried Robbie in her body, not in her arms, and it had all been so much simpler. Now it was going to be very hard. How could she snatch him away from everyone and everything he loved? But if she didn't...

"Charlie? Are you out there?"

Ernie entered the kitchen and she straightened, but her smile froze in place when she saw the picture in his hand.

He followed her gaze and waved it at her. "Yeah, I keep lookin' at this picture. It looks so familiar, you know? The guy who left it said he really had to find this girl. I'd like to help him out." He frowned, then looked at her. "I don't know who she is, but the people who are looking for her probably miss her a lot. I hope she gives them a call."

Something about the way he said that made her give him a sharp look, but his face was guileless. She bit her lip, not knowing what to say, and then, as though she'd been struck by lightning, an idea popped into her head. It was a crazy idea, a dangerous idea, an idea that couldn't possibly work. Could it?

But she didn't have much choice. She didn't have anywhere else to turn. She would have to start it out strong, and not look back, or it would never work. She had no time to think through the ramifications. The details would have to sort themselves out. She heard herself voicing it before she was even sure what exactly it was or where it had come from.

"To tell you the truth, I...uh, I had someone find me today." She swallowed hard and tried to smile again. "My...my husband showed up. After all these years."

Ernie gaped at her, the picture forgotten in his hand. "Robbie's dad?"

She nodded, wondering what Denver would say if he could hear this—afraid she probably knew. "Yes. He...uh...well, he rented a cabin near mine and showed up quite unexpectedly. I had no idea..."

Her voice trailed off and she bit her lip. She was going to have to do better than this.

"Wow, your husband." Ernie shook his head, troubled and obviously not sure if this was a good thing or a bad thing. "I thought you were through with him for good."

"I thought so too."

He frowned, thinking, and Charlie knew he was trying to remember everything she'd ever said about the man. He wouldn't remember much, because she'd played it cagey right from the beginning. She hadn't been sure how she was going to deal with it around Robbie, so she had purposely remained very vague with everyone who asked. Over time, everyone had lost interest anyway, and she'd never actually told anyone but her son any sort of definitive story.

"I'm not sure how it will work out, or if he'll stay very long. And one more thing," she added quickly. "Please don't tell Robbie. He doesn't know and I don't want him to get his hopes up in case things don't…you know…work out."

Ernie frowned, his good-natured face filled with confusion. "Do you mean the two of you might reconcile?"

She shrugged, knowing she was getting in deeper with every word, knowing she was lying to one of her very best friends. But right now, did she have a choice?

"You never know," she said weakly, avoiding his gaze and wincing as she thought of what Denver's face was going to look like when she presented this plan to him. "Stranger things have happened."

Ernie scratched his head. "That's wonderful, Charlie," he said doubtfully, as he turned back to his work. "I'm so glad."

She nodded, stunned at her own ability to weave a story out of thin air like this. These were people she'd never, ever lied to—if you didn't count that little thing about her name—and yet she was telling them stories like there was no tomorrow.

"You know what?" Ernie added, turning back from what he'd been doing and looking at her strangely. "I've just been thinking. You never go anywhere. You ought to take some time off. Why not take a few days and go off somewhere with this husband of yours? Michi and I could take care of Robbie for you. You could probably use some time to really get to know this guy again.''

Something caught in her throat and she bit her lip, then whirled, took a step and threw her arms around her friend. ''Ernie, I love you so,'' she said, tears welling in her eyes. ''You know what? I just might take you up on it.''

A few minutes later she was back at work, going through the stack of orders beginning to build at the order window, mechanically preparing to get something done. But all the time her mind was spinning off into space, working like a machine set on overdrive.

What had she done? This was crazy. But what else could she have done? She wouldn't go back and face her mother. She'd been under her mother's sway for too many years and she knew she wasn't strong enough to resist her control once she was in the same room with her. No, she wouldn't go back. She couldn't. She would do what she had to. If she could position herself as a married woman, even if someone noticed similarities between her and the picture—well, it might be dismissed as a coincidence. Then people might not get suspicious. She might have a chance to stay here where it was so good for her son.

The only thing was…what was Denver going to say?

Six

Denver was singing. It was something he didn't do very often and he wasn't particularly good at it. But he was doing it with gusto now, and he was really enjoying it.

He'd moped for a while after Charlie left him, glad to be alone, but bored, restless, unable to read or sleep or concentrate on anything productive. He'd kept his mind off her at any rate. That had been a small victory. He didn't want to think about her. He didn't want her to be anywhere near his thoughts. In fact, if he never saw her again...

Well, it was hard to say that, exactly. That might be going a little too far.

"Just as long as she stays out of my life," he'd told himself, and then he winced, because his leg was hurting like crazy.

He rummaged through the kitchen, but there were

no pain pills, not even aspirin. What he did find was a tall, shapely bottle of Scotch. He hesitated. He wasn't much of a drinker these days. But the leg throbbed and he knew the liquor could dull that a bit.

What the hell. Why not? It wasn't like he was going to be driving or even seeing another human being before daybreak. Why not have a few drinks? What could it hurt?

He sat down with a glass and the open bottle and let the first sweet sting slide down his throat. Sometimes it just felt so good. There weren't many things that felt better.

Except maybe a woman.

He swore softly. Why had he let his mind drift that way again? Charlie. She'd opened up areas in him that he'd closed and tried to seal against any lingering doubts. But somehow, the idea of having a woman in his life crept in.

He'd decided long ago that women weren't worth the cost. Not for him, at any rate. He'd heard there were some who were worth it. He'd seen happy marriages. At least, the couples said they were happy. But you never knew what really went on when the doors were closed, did you? And from his own experience, it was hard to give happiness in a long-term relationship much credence. There was just too much stacked against it.

His own parents had fought every night that he could remember, and when they'd died in a plane crash, it had almost been a relief that he wouldn't have to listen to that bickering any longer. He'd been young, barely nineteen, but he'd quickly taken over caring for his thirteen-year-old sister, going to work at two jobs until he could qualify for early admittance to the government program that led to the sort of under-cover espionage work he'd been doing for years now. He'd been determined to make a better life for Gail. He hadn't had the chance to finish college, but he swore she would, and he set out to make sure he could afford to send her to the best college prep school she could get into. Those were the days when he'd become used to taking risks. The dangerous assignments got the best pay, and the more pay accrued to him, the better he could care for Gail.

That day at her graduation, he'd been a happy man, knowing it had all been worthwhile. There she was, as lovely and educated as the wealthiest blue blood around, and already accepted at an Ivy League college. He'd done his duty by her, and then some. He was proud of that. Even despite what had come later—the horribly wrenching breach that had occurred between them when Gail had thrown it all away. The break with his sister still cut like a knife when he thought of it.

In the meantime, his own life had been a mess. During the first years with the agency, he hadn't really had time to date. Once the overseas assignments started coming, he'd come in contact with a lot of women, but they hadn't been the sort he would have wanted to bring home to meet his sister. And then there had been Mary.

He'd thought it was love. That just showed how young and naive he'd been at the time. She was beautiful, with silky black hair and huge blue eyes. She'd been a secretary at agency headquarters, and he'd fallen like a ton of bricks the minute he saw her. His heart beat so loud whenever he came near her, he didn't dare try to say anything for fear he wouldn't be able to hear himself speak. She'd smiled at him and that night, as he was eating dinner alone in the dining room of his hotel, there she was. She stopped to say hello, and one thing led to another. After that, he made it a point to stop in the District every chance he got, and she was always ready to see him. He'd lived in a fog, a soft, pink fog of infatuation, and he'd acted like a fool because of it. He'd been so sure this was it, the real thing, and that she was going to be the mother of his children. He even bought a ring. He had it with him the night he found her with another man in her apartment. His first instinct had been to kill the guy, but he was glad later that he'd controlled the impulse. It wasn't the guy's fault, after all. And in a way, it wasn't even hers. He'd found over the years that women were just like that. You couldn't depend on them. Any more than you could depend on men.

He knew better now. He didn't depend on anyone but himself. And it was better that way. People couldn't disappoint you if you didn't have any expectations. They couldn't rip your heart to shreds if you didn't hand it to them in the first place.

Now Charlie...there was a woman who he once would have thought was everything he'd ever dreamed of. He'd only seen her a few times all those years ago, but her image had stuck in his mind, and whenever he thought of ethereal perfection, her face had swum into view in his memories. She looked good, she moved with the grace of an angel, and she carried herself with a natural elegance that seemed to embody all the virtues you could want in a woman. He'd decided after that day of graduation that she was a snob, but he'd accepted that. He'd almost felt she had a right to be— as long as it didn't affect the way she treated Gail.

After all, she was born to it. Who could blame her if she felt a little above it all?

And now here she was, living in a dusty mountain valley filled with fishermen and lumberjacks, wearing jeans and working in a restaurant, just like any other young woman her age might. Had he been wrong about her from the beginning? Or was there something wrong with what she was doing here?

He shook his head and poured himself another drink. The answer was going to have to remain elusive, because he wasn't going to do a thing to find it out. Her face still haunted him, and now he could add that her body was a flame he didn't dare get too close to. All in all, she was murder. He didn't want any part of her. By the time most of the bottle of Scotch was gone, he'd decided that quite certainly. He was going to stay away from all women, but Charlie in particular.

And he'd thought of a nice song about it. Before he knew it, he was singing a few bars. And then the full concert began.

Charlie urged her little scooter on up the rocky hill toward the old McHenry place. Business had continued to be slow at the Pali and she'd been able to leave work early. Luckily, the man who'd left the picture hadn't returned and Ernie had urged her to go on home, encouraging her once again to take a few days off. Now she was racing to tell Denver that he was going to have to play the part of her husband. How she was going to break this extraordinary bit of news to him, she didn't really know.

"Say, Denver, would you mind being my long-lost husband for a few days? I would consider it a personal favor."

That approach wasn't going to work and she knew it. She was going to have to think of something, something to make him see how important this was to her without actually telling him any details. Was that possible? She didn't know, but she was going to have to try.

She turned off her engine and pulled the vehicle over to the side, expecting to see Denver in the doorway any moment. He couldn't have missed the sound of her arrival and she knew he wouldn't be pleased to see her. She thought he would appear only to wave her off, but when that didn't happen, she frowned and stopped to listen, her head cocked to the side. Someone was singing.

"Denver?" she said softly, her mouth twisting into a delighted grin. She made her way onto the porch as quietly as she could and peeked in through the window. Sure enough, there he was, sitting on the couch, his head back, his mouth moving. He was singing some old sad song from some ancient war and his face had the look of a man about to shed a bitter tear and maybe throw his glass into the fireplace, just for the pure emotion of it all.

She stared at him in wonder, and then she noticed the bottle. That cleared that one up. Shaking her head, she reached for the door knob and turned it, going on in without knocking.

He probably wouldn't have heard a knock anyway, because he didn't really notice her even when she stood in front of him. It was only when he finished his mournful song that he lowered his head and opened his eyes and saw her standing there with her arms crossed, looking down at him.

His first reaction was to grimace. "Oh, no. Not you again."

"Yes, it's me."

He shook his head, dismissing her out of hand, and his eyes were clouded with more than the liquor. "You're going to have to get over this need to mother me," he told her as firmly as he was able, though the slurring of his voice was a hindrance. "I don't need taking care of. I don't need any help." He waved his hand with the drink in it, amber liquid sloshing. "Go away."

She sighed with exasperation, her hands on her hips. This was a problem. He'd obviously had too much to drink. Not good. But she couldn't change the circumstances, so she supposed she might as well go ahead and deal with things the way they were.

"Calm down," she told him evenly. "I didn't come to mother you."

He half laughed. "Give me a break. You can't seem to help it. It must be some sort of Good Samaritan complex or something. You see yourself as some sort of angel of mercy, and…"

The picture he was painting stung a little bit, but she pushed that aside. "No," she told him quickly. "I assure you, this time my reasons are completely self-ish."

He blinked as he gazed up at her, seemingly impressed with her sincerity. "They are?"

She nodded, jaw set with determination. "I came for *me,* not for *you.*"

"Oh." He hesitated, frowning as though he wasn't quite sure what to think, then shrugged, his shoulders relaxing as he did so. "Well, I guess that's okay, then."

Her mouth twitched. She would have laughed out loud, only she was sure that would have offended him, so she bit her tongue and dropped down to sit on the couch beside him, looking at him sideways. He needed a shave, his hair was rumpled attractively and his body language had lost the ramrod stiffness he'd had that afternoon. All in all, she was afraid she rather liked him inebriated. He seemed a little more human.

"What do you have against being taken care of?" she asked him, just to make conversation—and to put off the subject she was going to have to raise very soon.

It was the wrong thing to dwell on. Even as she said the words, she noted a little of the stiffness reappearing.

"I don't need to be taken care of," he said curtly, looking disgruntled. "*I* am the one who takes care of things."

She knew it wasn't wise to challenge someone she was about to ask a favor of, but she couldn't help it. "Ah," she said wisely. "So it all boils down to the fact that you're a control freak."

His brows drew together. "No. It's not that."

She leaned toward him, leading with her chin, pinning him with her violet gaze. "What are you afraid of? That you'll owe me something?"

He pulled back, frowning. "I don't owe you anything. I chopped wood, remember?"

She raised one eyebrow, not letting up on him. "And you think that makes up for all the nurturing I did? The dry clothes. The pot roast. And the cherry pie?"

He was beginning to look worried. "What do you want?" he asked her.

She gave him a superior look. "You owe me."

His frown grew more fierce and he rubbed his stubbled chin with the back of his hand. "I don't owe you anything."

"Yes, you do." She paused, letting the horror sink in. "Want to know how you can pay me back?" she finally added softly.

He gave a mirthless laugh. "Here we go. What is it?"

She moved a bit closer to him on the couch. "Just a little favor."

He leaned back away, looking at her with narrowed eyes. "What lil' favor?"

She gave him her most winning smile. "It would really help me out if you would...." She took a deep breath and batted her eyelashes demurely, then let it out in a rush. "If you would pretend to be my husband. Just for a little while. Hardly any time at all. I really, really need this."

He stared at her for a long moment, then drew back away from her as far as the end of the couch would let him. "Oh, no you don't," he said, slurring his words only slightly and looking at her as though she might grow snakes out of her head at any moment. "You stay away from me."

But she reached for him, putting a hand on his arm, holding him lightly. "Wait, Denver, I..."

He winced and stared down at where she was touching him, as though she might have something that was catching. "Uh-uh," he said, shaking his head.

Her fingers tightened. She was so sure he would read the earnest appeal in her eyes and be unable to resist helping her. "You don't understand. I don't mean anything physical. Or even emotional. I just need you to tell people we're married.''

''No.'' With his free hand, he tossed the rest of his drink down his throat and made a face as it burned its way down. ''It's impossible,'' he managed to grind out around the fire.

She scooted closer, just to make sure he couldn't get away, her fingers curling into the fabric of his shirtsleeve. ''It's not impossible.'' She smiled again, coaxing him. ''Hey, come on. We would make a great couple, don't you think?''

He stared at her searchingly, his gaze looking deeply into her eyes in a way that made her breath come a little faster. ''No,'' he said at last, drawing the word out. He shook his head as though to clear it, as though he finally saw through to the heart of her request. ''No.'' A sense of new outrage suddenly filled his eyes and he looked back into her face as though he'd just stopped something dastardly in its tracks. ''No, thank you very much, but I don't want to get married.''

She frowned. ''No, Denver, wait...''

He put a hand out as though to hold her off, touching her shoulder. ''You're a beautiful woman,'' he proclaimed as though making a speech. ''But I don't want kids and I don't like being tied down.'' He shook his head. ''Marriage is not for me. So forget about it.''

He turned away. The case was obviously closed.

She threw up her hands in exasperation. What was the matter with the man? She thought she'd explained all this pretty clearly. And here he seemed to think she was proposing. And...she stared at him as she realized this...he was turning her down. And rather insultingly at that.

Her eyes flashed. "Hey, mister, I don't care if you don't want to really get married. Nobody asked you. I was merely…"

He gave her a long-suffering look as though to say, "Don't try to kid a kidder." Out loud he said, "You were asking me just now."

"I…" She sputtered, outraged and half embarrassed at the same time. "If I wanted to get married, really married, there are a lot of men I would rather marry than you, believe me."

"Oh, yeah?" He turned so that he was looking deep into her eyes again, looking in that way that seemed to curl her toes. "Oh, yeah?" he repeated, leaning closer as if to intimidate, but coming across as seductive instead, his gaze deepening until he seemed to be melting into her. She stared back, and something that had begun to quiver deep inside her earlier began to quiver again.

"Yeah," she said back, but her voice was more breathless than she would have liked it to be, and her heart was pounding so loudly, she was afraid he would hear it.

And then he touched her cheek with his finger, let it linger, and suddenly his eyes were haunted by shadows, swirling with mystery, and he was looking at her mouth. "You might change your mind if I kissed you," he suggested softly.

"I seriously doubt it," she claimed, though the effort took all the concentration she could muster.

And she didn't move away. Even when he curled her into his arm and began to draw her closer, she didn't protest.

She wasn't sure why she didn't. After all, it had been years since a man had been successful with her, in any way at all. She'd had men try. She'd usually managed to hold them off with sharp words, but occasionally a slap or a good hard push had been involved. Her firm response had made sure no man's lips had touched hers in over five years. So why didn't she put up a fight when Denver pulled her up against his chest and breathed in the scent of her hair?

She felt sort of like she was swimming in honey. Everything seemed to go in slow motion, but it felt so good. Sort of golden. She couldn't think. She couldn't say a word. When she tried to move, her arms wouldn't work. She was…sort of helpless. It was almost like she'd been drugged.

He smelled like liquor and soap and something indefinable—something male and deliciously dangerous. She turned into his kiss as though she'd been kissing him all her life, but as his mouth closed on hers, everything changed, rocketing out of control. That little melting area inside turned volcanic, filling her with surging heat. She felt as though she were opening, growing, expanding, releasing a part of herself that had been chained up and starving. His mouth was hot and sweet and she wanted more of it, pressing herself to him, letting her fingers tangle in his thick hair, pulling him closer. There was an urgency inside her that she'd never known before, an instinct to find a way to get closer still, to burrow into him, to have him in her.

She wanted him. This was new to her and instead of fearing it, she was ready to throw away caution and plunge in. In a matter of seconds she went from wary observer to sensual participant, and she didn't stop to look back.

But he did.

Despite his advanced state of intoxication, he sensed

exactly what was happening to her and he knew he could take her. She was so good, so beautiful, so ready, he felt desire grow and overcome his physical state. Experience told him that despite the liquor, his body was ready; instinct told him she would accept him; his libido told him to take this offering and enjoy it; his sense of self-preservation told him to back away quick; and his conscience told him he was acting like a jerk.

She was much too vulnerable. From what she'd said, from what he could sense, he knew she'd been without a man for years, and for some strange reason, she'd picked him to lower her guard with. This wasn't the time, wasn't the place. If he did this to her now, he would regret it. This wasn't right.

But it was growing late. Things were approaching the point of no return. In the groggy state he was in, if he didn't watch out, his body would take over and let his conscience rot. It was time to take care of business.

He tried to pull away, but she followed him, her hands sliding under his shirt, pushing it away, her palms pressing on the muscles of his chest, as though she could mold him. Her touch felt good, too good. He groaned deep down and fought himself for control. It was slipping away, and every minute he stayed with her, it was getting harder and harder to imagine leaving her alone. He had to do something. Anything to stop this. And then he turned, deliberately, and landed on his bad leg.

Pain shot through him and he jerked with it, gasping. She sprang away, crying out in remorse and he lay back, his eyes closed, and waited for the pain to ebb. He was vaguely aware that she was helping him up, directing him to his bed. The pain faded rather quickly, but the regret fogged his mind like a dismal night along the shore. He'd had a chance to have the woman who had filled his dreams for years, and he'd thrown it away. Was he nuts? Or just very, very confused?

Maybe both. He groaned and lay back as she pulled the covers up over him, closing his eyes, fighting back the dizziness. He heard movement in the room and he turned his head. "Charlyne?" he asked groggily. "Are you still here?"

She froze, her back to him, her hand on the doorknob. Her eyes widened and she turned slowly to stare at him. "What did you say?"

He opened his eyes and blinked at the ceiling, then rose on one elbow, wincing, to look at her. "I said your name. Adrianna Charlyne Chandler. Wasn't that it?"

She drew her arms around her, holding tightly, and then she shivered. She hadn't heard it spoken aloud for so many years. It touched her to hear it, like the sound of an old beloved melody. She looked at him, her eyes huge in the darkened room. "Are you the one?" she asked quietly. "Did my mother send you?"

He stared at her blankly. "Your mother?" he repeated. He shook his head as though trying to clear it and understand what she was saying. "What does your mother have to do with anything?"

She drew in her breath and held it, then let it go. "Who are you?"

He tried to focus on her and failed, laying his head back down on the pillow. "McCaine is my real last name," he told her wearily. "My sister Gail was a friend of yours in school."

Gail McCaine. Denver McCaine. She stared at him, a shadowy picture surfacing of a long-ago day at graduation when Gail's rough-looking and extremely attractive brother had appeared and then disappeared so quickly. She'd noticed him then, noticed him in the way a girl that age notices a special sort of man, and now she knew where the feeling of having met him before had come from.

"Denver McCaine," she repeated softly, coming to stand over him at the edge of the bed, examining every feature of his face. "Oh, my God. I can't believe it."

He opened his eyes. The room spun for a moment, then slowed down, and he saw her blond hair swaying above him. He reached out and caught hold of it, curling it around his hand as though it would anchor him to safety.

"Stay with me," he whispered to her, pulling her toward him with her own hair. "Stay. I won't...do anything. I promise. Please stay."

He kept drawing her nearer, though now he wasn't sure if he was really doing it, or dreaming. But as he was drifting toward sleep he could feel her climbing in beside him. The sense of peace it gave him was sweeter even than the lovemaking could have been. He lay back and let sleep take him.

She watched him in the moonlight. His breathing was slow and deep. It had been an hour or so since he'd fallen asleep, but she couldn't get up and leave him, although she knew she should.

Denver McCaine. Something about that name delighted her, linked her to a past she'd run from, but still felt a part of. She wanted to talk all night, find out what had happened to people they both knew, find out about Gail. But that would have to wait until he'd slept off the alcohol. Until then, she could enjoy seeing him, listening to him breathe.

Funny. It had never been this way with Jeff. Bedtime had usually been a stormy, unhappy part of the day. She'd never lain awake and watched him sleep. She'd never even thought of doing anything like that. Why was it different with Denver?

She thought back over the times she'd seen him when she was a teenager. She'd always wondered about him. Gail had been a sweet girl, and her brother had looked so…rough. But now that she thought back, she knew there had been something disturbing about the way he'd looked at her, even then.

Chemistry. She'd thought it was a hoax, but now she wasn't so sure. She and Denver had chemistry, if that was what those sparks were all about.

Suddenly, she was grinning in the dark of night. Of course, it didn't mean a thing. But it certainly was fun.

Still, she ought to go. She really should. She knew she shouldn't be here. She was a mother. She had a child to think about. It wasn't right to be in a man's bed this way. She'd never in a thousand years imagined she would do such a thing as she was doing now.

Turning half way, she stretched luxuriously and when she turned back, she found herself pressing her face against his shoulder and she sighed. This was it—contact. The most dangerous element of all. She knew she should jump back like a scalded cat. But his flesh felt so warm, so smooth, so hard. The rounded bulge of his shoulder muscle had magic to it, drawing her closer. He felt like heaven and she breathed in the scent of his skin, let her lips touch it, closed her eyes and reveled in the sense of male presence she'd been missing for so long.

"It isn't really him," she told herself groggily. "It's just his maleness. I just need to touch him..."

Night closed in around like a velvet fog, and she slept. But her sleep was light and she dreamed of making love. The man was obscure. She couldn't see his face. But his body looked a lot like the one she clung to. And the sense of peace from his lovemaking filled her like a spring day full of sunbeams.

Seven

Charlie stirred. A man's arms held her and she didn't want to leave them, but there was a knocking, and it went on and on....

Her eyes shot open. Before she even remembered where she was she realized what the knocking meant. There was someone at the door.

"Someone's at the door," she murmured, pulling away from the comforting embrace and blinking in the silvery rays of first morning light. This wasn't her bed. This wasn't her house. Suddenly she realized where she was and why.

"Oh, my God," she whispered, staring down at Denver.

His eyes were barely slits but he looked as shocked as she was and his body tensed. "What the hell...?" he began.

But she didn't wait to hear what he was asking.

Rolling away from him she was thankful for only one thing: at least they both still had their clothes on. More or less. One glance at Denver's beautiful chest made her wince, but that wasn't important.

Someone was still at the door and a voice came in loud and clear.

"Charlie? Are you in there?"

Margo. Charlie held her breath and closed her eyes for a moment. There was no escape. Her friend and neighbor Margo was here and she wasn't going to go away easily.

Denver was up on his elbow but he was still staring at her with the look of a man who had never seen her before in his life. Maybe he didn't remember why she was here. Maybe he didn't remember anything at all about last night. How interesting—but irrelevant at the moment.

"It's Margo, my neighbor," she explained, gesticulating as though that would make him understand the words more clearly. "Don't you get it? She's here. There's no way to avoid her."

"Don't answer the door," he suggested, though he was still frowning in puzzlement—as if he thought Charlie had appeared in a spaceship on his roof and come down the chimney, and he had no responsibility for her being here at all.

"I have to," she hissed back at him, straightening her clothes. "She's seen my scooter. She knows I'm here."

He stared at her for a few seconds more, then closed his eyes. "Make her go away," he muttered.

She knew he meant the same for her, too—that he wished she would disappear just as much as he wished Margo would. But she ignored that.

"Making her go away is no easy chore with my friend Margo," she told him as she looked into the mirror and ran a hand through her hair. "But I'll do what I can."

He didn't speak or move or make any other sign that he'd heard, and she left the room, running quickly to the door and throwing it open.

"Hi, Margo," she said, managing a cheerful smile. "What on earth are you doing here at the crack of dawn?"

Margo tried to answer but her astonishment got the better of her and nothing came out but a soft gurgle. Brian, her husband, was standing behind her, looking embarrassed and as though he'd rather be almost anywhere else.

"Wh...what are you doing here?" Margo demanded when she'd found her voice. Then she threw up her hands. "No, I take that back, don't tell me!"

Charlie tried to laugh but didn't quite manage it. "Margo," she began, but her friend wasn't in the mood to listen.

"Charlie, I've been searching for you since last night. I called your house and you weren't home. You're always home." She frowned as though this was something that really should be explained right away. "I needed you for some advice about a dessert I was planning. You're the only one I know who can cook desserts decently and I really wanted to talk to you."

Charlie gave her a wavery smile. "I'm sorry, Margo. I..."

"Well, the kids told me they'd seen some man hauling you off on your scooter yesterday. I couldn't imagine how that could have been, but then someone called late last night and said they'd seen your scooter parked outside the old McHenry place. I said, no, that just can't be, but you never did come home and there I was tossing and turning all night, worrying about you, and finally I said, 'Brian, we have to go rescue her if I'm ever going to be able to sleep again.'" She waved an arm as she gazed sharply into the house, searching the shadows for the enemy she was sure lurked there somewhere. "Is there really a man? Don't worry, honey. Brian can deal with him. Where is he? Brian will take care of him, won't you, Brian?"

It seemed to Charlie that Brian had a desperate look in his eyes as he tried to calm his wife. "Uh, Margo, I don't know about this. I mean, Charlie is a grown woman. If she wants to…"

But Margo wasn't listening. She reached for Charlie's hand and tugged. "Come on, let's you and me go," she ordered stoutly. "We'll take you home where you belong. And if you want to file charges…"

"Margo, stop it." Charlie was half laughing, but more in despair than amusement. "The man you're talking about didn't bring me here against my will. I came on my own."

Margo didn't want to hear any excuses and she looked very stern. "There's more than one way to skin a cat, Charlie, and there's more than one way to seduce a woman. Pretty words can be as powerful as strong rope for some men. We'll get you out of here and when you can think straight, you'll thank…"

"Margo, listen to me," Charlie said, getting tough herself. "I'm here on my own. I want to be here."

Margo's hands went to her hips and her head went back. "Is that so? Well, I don't believe it. I know you, Charlie Smith, and I know you wouldn't go off…"

ome closer still
Silhouette with
wo FREE books and
welcome gift

PEEL
OFF

PLACE
INSIDE

How to claim your two FREE books and welcome gift

If you've enjoyed reading this new book, then this is your opportunity to get even closer still to Silhouette Desire® and enjoy two more free books and a welcome gift. This is all you have to do.

1. **Peel off the free gift seal** from the front cover. Place it in the space provided to the right. This automatically entitles you to receive two free books and a lovely silvertone heart necklace.

2. **Complete your details** on the card, detach it along the dotted line, and post it back to us. No stamp needed. We'll then send you two selected romances from the Desire™ series, yours to keep absolutely FREE.

3. **Enjoy the read.** We hope that after receiving your free books you'll want to remain a subscriber. But the choice is yours – to continue or cancel, any time at all! So why not accept our no risk invitation? You'll be glad you did.

Your satisfaction is guaranteed

You are under no obligation to buy anything. We charge you nothing for your introductory parcel. And you don't have to make any minimum number of purchases – not even one! Thousands of readers have already discovered that the Reader Service is the most convenient way of enjoying the latest new romance novels before they are available in the shops. Of course, post and packing is completely FREE.

Jane Nicholls

Yours FREE...
when you reply today

This elegant necklace is classically styled with an exquisite heart pendant presented on a generous 18" silvertone chain. Respond today and it's all yours.

YES. Please send me my two FREE books and welcome gift

YES. I have placed my free gift seal in the space provided above. Please send me two free books and my welcome gift. I understand that I am under no obligation to purchase any books, as explained on the back and on the opposite page. I am over 18 years of age.

BLOCK CAPITALS   D0AI

Ms/Mrs/Miss/Mr   Initials

Surname

Address

_____

_____
                                                            Postcode
_____

Thank you!

Offer valid in UK only and is not available to subscribers to the Desire series. Overseas readers please write for details. We reserve the right to refuse an application and applicants must be aged 18 years or over. Only one application per household. Terms and prices subject to change. As a result of this application you may receive further offers from Harlequin Mills & Boon Ltd. and other carefully selected companies. If you do not want to share in this opportunity please write to the Data Manager at the address overleaf. Offer expires 31st July 2000.

Silhouette is a registered trademark, used under license. Desire is being used as a trademark.

Detach and keep your complimentary bookmark ▸

How The Reader Service works

Accepting free books and gifts places you under no obligation to buy anything. You may keep the books and gift and return the despatch note marked "cancel". If we don't hear from you, about a month later we will send you four new Desire™ novels and invoice you for just £2.70 each. That's the complete price – there is no extra charge for postage and packing. You may cancel at any time, otherwise every month we'll send you four more books which you may purchase or return – the choice is yours.

SILHOUETTE DESIRE®
FREE BOOK OFFER
FREEPOST CN81
CROYDON
CR9 3WZ

NO
STAMP
NEEDED

Words stopped in her throat because Denver chose that moment to come into the room, shrugging into his shirt as he came, his eyes cool but bleary, his hair combed and face washed. They all turned to stare at him and for just a moment, even Charlie was tongue-tied. Even with a hangover, he looked good enough to hang a crush on any day.

"Good morning," he said evenly, glancing from one of them to the other. "What can I do for you?"

Charlie turned back to her friends and tried to smile. "This is…uh…Denver Smith."

"Smith?" Margo turned to her in surprise. "Did you say 'Smith'?"

Charlie nodded. "Yes. He's my…husband."

"Your what?" Both of them turned to stare at Denver and Denver turned to stare at Charlie and Charlie felt her heart lurch and she began to talk very fast, her voice steady but a little high-pitched.

"Denver is my husband. You knew I had one, didn't you? He's…Robbie's father. We broke up years ago, before Robbie was born, and I came here to live and now he came to see if…if maybe we could get back together again, so we're talking and mulling it over and wondering what we should do, so you see, we really needed some time alone to work things out and…"

Margo was the first to react. True to her nature as the queen of mood swings, she was filled with sudden remorse. "Oh. Oh, Charlie, I'm so sorry. Why didn't you tell me?"

"Why didn't you tell *me?*" Denver asked also, but his words went unheard as Margo's voice went on and on. Charlie looked into his eyes and shook her head, giving him a weak and wavering smile. From the look

on his face she was afraid he didn't remember anything about last night—or about her request that he
play make-believe for a little while.

"I'm sorry," she told him softly. "As soon as they
go I'll explain."

Unfortunately, getting them headed back down the
mountain took some doing. Margo wanted to join in
celebrating something that hadn't happened and it was
confusing for her to come to terms that nobody seemed
willing to answer her friendly and well-meaning questions. She finally left reluctantly, dragging her puzzled
husband along, and Charlie turned to face Denver
again.

He looked as solid as a stone wall and just as im-
movable, like something carved by an ancient Greek.
She smiled at him, but he didn't smile back, and she
turned nervously away.

"It looks like your leg is getting better," she said
quickly, putting off the inevitable as long as she could.

His mouth twisted. "Yup. It's a lot better. There's
no excuse for you to stick around and nursemaid me."

She gazed at him quickly, wondering where that
lovely man she'd been with the night before had gone.
She knew he was still in there somewhere, but she
suspected Denver wasn't going to let him out again if
he could help it.

"More's the pity," she murmured.

"What?"

"Nothing." She smiled at him. "Would you like
some coffee?" she suggested brightly. "I'll just go in
the kitchen and brew us some…"

Denver caught hold of her arm before she could get
past him. "I don't want any coffee," he said bluntly.
"What I want is an explanation."

She spent a moment searching his deep blue eyes before she replied. He wasn't in a very good mood. The suspicious mountain man had returned. His fingers were gripping her arm in an unfriendly way and much as she liked being this close to him, she knew it wasn't going to help. She still had to settle this thing about pretending to be married.

She glanced at him nervously. He wasn't going to go for it. Not the way he was looking at her, as though she'd found a chink in his armor and he couldn't tolerate anyone doing that. A straightforward request wasn't going to do any good at all, she could see that. She was going to have to find another way.

She made a quick examination of his handsome face, then centered her gaze on his eyes again. "I wouldn't have thought you were a drinker," she said softly, in hopes of changing the subject.

It worked for the moment. He dropped his hand from her arm as though he'd been stung. "I'm not a drinker," he protested.

"Really?" She threw him a coy look and went on into the kitchen. "You were doing a pretty good imitation of one last night," she said over her shoulder as she went.

He followed her, standing stiffly in the doorway while she began to wash out the coffeepot she found draining in the sink before reaching for the coffee can at the back of the counter. She worked at preparing everything just perfectly, trying not to let on how nervous she felt, ready to jump sky-high the moment he spoke, but when he still didn't say anything, she looked back at him and found his eyes were more troubled than she'd ever seen them before.

"What else did I do last night?" he asked her softly,

and she swallowed the gasp that rose in her throat, realizing he really wasn't sure.

"You mean you don't remember?" she asked, gazing at him wide-eyed.

He tried to look confident. "Sure," he said with unconvincing heartiness. "I remember everything." But his deep blue eyes searched hers for clues. "I was just wondering…well, how you felt about…it."

She held onto the counter and wanted to laugh out loud. He didn't remember. He wasn't sure what they'd done—what *he'd* done. She turned away to measure out the ground coffee, thinking about this situation and barely hiding her smile. The tough guy was uncertain how to proceed. A part of her wanted to take him in her arms, reassure him, let him know there was nothing to worry about at all. But she wasn't going to let herself do that. There were other things to think about. Right now, there was her future and what she needed from him. Did she have the nerve to tease him a little longer?

She put on the water to boil and turned back to where he was waiting. His eyes were still unsure. She smiled at him.

"You want to know how I feel about it?" she repeated slowly, acting just a little shy. "Couldn't you tell? Last night, I mean."

A muscle twitched at his temple and he reached out to prop himself up against the counter. "I…well, no," he admitted.

Her eyes were huge with seeming innocence. "It was so sudden. I mean, I know we should have gotten to know each other better before we…before we…"

He swallowed hard and steeled himself before he asked her, "Before we what?"

She sighed happily turning to look out the window at the pines. "Got so serious," she said shyly.

"Serious?" He was pulling at the neck of his shirt as though it was too tight. "I'm never serious," he added quickly. "That's something you've got to realize about me. You haven't really gotten to know me well enough. I'm joking all the time. I—I never mean what I say."

"You meant this," she told him confidently. "A man has to mean what he says in the middle of…" She glanced at him sideways and shrugged. "Well, you know."

He started to swear, then stopped himself. "No," he said quickly instead, moving closer, looking very intense. "No, I don't know. Tell me what you mean."

She poured him a mug of coffee instead and looked up as she handed it to him. "I've never had a man say something like that to me before," she told him as she picked up her own mug and started for the front room.

He watched her go for a moment, a small frown appearing between his brows. Then he followed her silently, dropping down to sit next to her at the little table where she settled. He searched her eyes for a moment, as though he were searching for an answer he couldn't find, and then he said, "Listen, Charlie. I was drunk. I didn't know what I was saying. In fact I…well, I don't really remember what I said."

"Too bad," she said, teasing him with a flirtatious smile. "It was quite a speech. You were very persuasive last night."

He blanched, cupping the hot mug in his hands and hunching over it with a groan. But before she had a chance to feel too smug, his face cleared and he looked up at her.

"Wait a minute," he said, blinking at her. "Wait a minute. I wasn't that drunk." He frowned at her suspiciously. "Pieces of last night are coming back to me. There was something about..." His eyes darted toward her and then away again, and he frowned. "There was something about...about people getting married, and then this morning you said..."

If his memory was coming back, it was time to strike. She leaned forward and said quickly, "You don't remember asking me to marry you last night?"

He stared at her for a moment, deer-in-the-headlights style, and then he made a face and shook his head. He could see through her game now. Very funny. But also very out of character. "Oh, no," he said, his natural self-confidence reasserting itself. "No." He sat back and shook his head. "No, that's just impossible."

She sighed, gazing at him with regret. It had been fun while it had lasted. "There you go again," she told him, ready to squeeze the last drop of advantage from the situation. "You don't really remember. Listen, I'll tell you exactly what happened." Abandoning her mug, she leaned toward him. "You were very seductive. You were trying to prove to me that I could fall for a guy like you. That I could be attracted to you."

He drew back. He was on firmer footing now and he wasn't buying it any longer. But he had to admit, she'd had him going for a few minutes. "Why did that need proving?" he said out of the corner of his mouth.

Her eyes widened. "Oh, I suppose you think it's obvious?"

"Damn right." His eyes were sparkling with amusement now. "Any fool could have seen that. You've had a thing for me from the beginning."

Her mouth dropped open and she started to laugh. "You...you..."

"All those phony reasons to get me out of my clothes," he went on, teasing her as mercilessly as she'd been teasing him. "Finding every excuse you could to stick around. Pure unadulterated lust. Anyone could have seen you were a goner."

"Denver!"

She reached out as though to slap him and he grabbed her hand and yanked her closer.

"Looking for ways to force physical contact," he added, giving her some, then circling her wrist with his fingers and holding it up as evidence.

She was laughing, shaking her head at his outrageous charges, and then, suddenly, she seemed to see something in his eyes and she went very still, her face only inches from his. He could feel her breath against his face—he could taste it. A strand of blond hair was falling down over her eyes and her lips looked as bright red as strawberries and something inside him turned hot and hungry and it seemed a natural thing when he leaned down and kissed her softly on the mouth.

"Are you trying to deny it?" he murmured against her lips. "Come on. Say that you want me."

Breathless, she shook her head, but her gaze said he was right, and he kissed her again, her lips soft as a spring breeze against his, so soft he had to open his eyes to make sure he wasn't dreaming that she was still there.

Her eyes were closed, her dark lashes lying against

her high cheekbones. Everything in her lovely face said surrender. Every vibe coming from her said she was his for the asking. An ache began to grow inside him, grow and spread and fill him with agony. To give her up was to bring on physical pain, but he knew he had to do it. Once he reminded himself of who they were—of who he was, of who she was, he knew he had no real choice.

He drew back, dropping her hand, reaching for his coffee as though that would save him, and she looked up, startled, wondering why. He pushed the coffee away. That wasn't going to do the trick. He had to get out of there or he would kiss her again. Lurching to his feet, he started for the front door. The sun was barely up. Maybe he'd go out and see it rise in the sky. He walked as quickly as he could on his injured leg across the front porch and out onto the bark path. She was coming behind him, and a part of him wished she wouldn't. The other part could only think about kissing her again.

He reached a broken-down stone wall and hesitated. The view of the valley was pretty nice, and he slumped down to sit on the wall. She sat, too, although he noticed, cynically, that it was as far away as she could get from him. They sat quietly for a long moment, then he spoke.

"Okay, give it to me straight," he said gruffly. "Did we or did we not make love last night?"

She hesitated, only a moment, then turned to smile at him. "So you really think I'm 'that kind of girl'?" she responded lightly, evading the direct question. "You think I would hop into bed with a man I hardly know?"

He looked up and met her bright gaze. "I don't

know why not. You were in my bed when I woke up this morning, weren't you?''

She sighed, her shoulders sagging, and drew her arms around her knees, looking out over the tops of the pines. ''Okay, here's what happened last night. You had too much to drink. I came in and asked you to help me with something. You agreed, and in the process, we sort of…well, we kissed and stuff.'' She glanced at him sideways, but he showed no reaction and she went on breezily. ''Then we talked about getting married and you said it might be a good idea…''

Now he reacted. ''You little liar! I know I didn't do that.'' He said it firmly, surely, leaving no more room for uncertainty. The kidding was over.

She threw up her hands. ''Okay, okay. You didn't actually ask me to marry you last night. But you did agree to *pretend* that we're married.''

He frowned skeptically, looking at her. ''Did I?''

She hesitated, avoiding looking directly into his gaze. ''Why not? After it turned out we're old friends…''

''I did tell you I recognized you? I'm not dreaming that part?''

She nodded. ''Yes. And it was a shock.'' Her head rose. ''Say, how is Gail, anyway? I haven't heard from her—or anyone—for a long, long time.''

He moved restlessly where he sat. ''I don't know,'' he said shortly. ''Gail and I have no contact right now.''

She stared at him. He shook his head and turned away. Obviously, he didn't want to talk about it. She hesitated. She wanted to hear more but there were too many other things on her plate at the moment, and she decided news about Gail would have to wait.

"Okay. Whatever. But as I was saying, we're old friends and so…" She took a deep breath and turned to face him. "Listen, you know my real name isn't Smith. I'm using that name because I don't want anyone to find me here. You found me by accident, I know, but I'm hoping we can keep it that way. It's really important. I…I sort of ran away from home almost six years ago."

Now she had his complete attention. He stared at her, waiting for more.

"I came here to the mountains when I was about to have Robbie. Michiko and Ernie—the people who run the Pali, where I work—they took me in and looked after me. They are my best friends in the whole world. I'm staying here. I won't go back, no matter what."

Denver glanced at her hand, looking for the ring he already knew wasn't there. He wanted to ask her about Robbie's father, but he didn't. He just waited for her to go on with her story.

"Okay," she said, leaning toward him with an earnest look on her pretty face. "Here's the deal. You are the only person in town who knows who I really am. Nobody from my past knows where I am. Not family. Not old friends. Nobody. I have a completely new life here and that's the way it has to be."

He reached up and ran his hand through his hair, grimacing. He wasn't sure just why it was, but some instinct told him this wasn't right, that she shouldn't be doing this. "What's the problem with contacting your family? Don't you think they would like to hear from you?"

Her gaze shifted. "I've let them know that I'm okay," she said quickly. "But I can't have any other contact." She glanced back at him. "Do you remember my mother at all? Do you remember what she's like? She ruined my life for twenty-one years and she's not going to get a chance to ruin Robbie's.''

Her voice rose as she spoke. He heard the emotion building and he looked down at his hands. ''So you're hiding up here under an assumed name and your little boy doesn't even know his grandmother,'' he said quietly.

She nodded, turning her head away and looking toward the window.

''Is that fair?'' he asked her.

''Of course not,'' she snapped, whipping her head back. ''Life isn't fair, is it? But things have to be this way.'' She pushed back her hair with an impatient gesture, then took a deep breath and calmed herself. ''When he's eighteen, I'll introduce them,'' she added, trying for a light tone but not quite bringing it off.

He shook his head. ''This is crazy,'' he said flatly.

''It may be crazy, but it is my life.'' She glanced at him, noting one of the many scars he had on his arm. ''And from what I've seen of you, you don't have much right to talk. You live a pretty crazy life yourself, don't you?''

''That's my choice. But I'm the only one who has to live with the consequences.''

She winced. ''Okay, I get the implied criticism, and to some extent, I deserve it. But I've got to raise my son the way I think is best. And I'm not going to allow my mother to come up here and haul us back to San Francisco, which is exactly what would happen if she knew where I was.'' She reached out impulsively and took his hand in hers. ''And now there's some detective she's hired snooping around town, leaving my picture all over the place. Luckily it's an old picture and no one has connected it with me so far.'' She looked into his eyes. ''But I need insurance. I need to have a husband around. Then no one will connect me with the missing woman. I won't fit the description at all. And that's where you come in.'' Her smile was winning. ''We went over some of this last night. You just don't remember.''

He liked her smile. He always had. ''So you're telling me I agreed to be your pretend husband last night,'' he said slowly.

She nodded, looking out over the scenery. ''Sure. Why not? You did.''

He turned his hand, capturing hers and pulling her around to face him. ''Look me in the eye and say that,'' he demanded.

''Denver!'' She tried to tug her hand away.

''Right straight in the eye.''

Her head rose slowly. ''Don't you believe me?''

He gave a half laugh. ''Why should I believe you? You've done nothing but lie to me all morning.''

Her chin rose and she bit her lip. ''Strong words,'' she murmured, her eyes troubled.

''But accurate.'' He dropped her hand and leaned back. ''Wouldn't you say?''

She sighed, rubbing her wrist where his hand had been. ''Okay. I'm just fibbing a little. You didn't actually promise. But I told you that you owed me, and you didn't—well, you didn't say no in so many words.''

He stared at her, fascinated. If anyone had told him just the day before that he would be contemplating pretending to be married to Charlyne Chandler—but that was just it. The pretending part. Charlie was asking him to be her hired hand, and that was all he would ever be to her. Well, he wasn't going to do it.

"Be serious, Charlie. You're a grown woman. Go back and face your mother."

"I can't." She shook her head, looking out over the scenery again. "I really can't do that."

His mouth quirked. "Then we're a pair, I guess. Because I can't help you."

She went on as though she hadn't heard him. "You wouldn't have to do anything, really. You wouldn't have to come and live with me or anything like that...."

He shook his head. "Charlie, did it ever occur to you that I came here for my own set of reasons? That I might not want too many people to know I'm here?"

She closed her eyes, but only for a moment. Then she rose and started for the house. "It's too bad, really," she said over her shoulder, her words floating back to him. "We would have made a great couple."

He sat where he was and let the words sink in. He heard her start up her scooter and drive off, but he didn't watch. He was seeing her again as she'd looked that day at his sister's graduation. It was a vision he'd held close over the years. Maybe it was time to let it go.

Charlie was packing. Things were in a mess. The way she saw it, she had two choices. She could either stay here and face the music—and her mother's investigator when he zeroed in on her—or she could get out of town for a while and hope this would all blow over before the time she got back.

That was it—a vacation. Why not? She and Robbie had never gone on a trip. They could take a vacation somewhere. People took them all the time. People went to Florida, for heaven's sake. South America. France. She and Robbie could go—where? They wouldn't get far on her scooter, but she did have some money saved up. They would have to take the bus. Good—most detectives headed straight for airports to catch you, didn't they? She and Robbie would be on the bus. No one would ever think of that.

She would cut her hair short, maybe dye it. She could dress Robbie as a little girl. She burst into laughter at that point, seeing Robbie's tough little face in a bonnet in her mind's eye. Maybe not. That wouldn't really work too well. They would just have to take their chances.

The best hope was probably the bus to Reno and then the train from there. "Get out of town, before it's too late, my love," she sang as she rummaged through Robbie's toys, throwing the good ones in one pile, the tired and threadbare in another.

She'd come home just in time to greet her son as the Howells dropped him off. Once they'd waved goodbye to their friends, she turned to Robbie and told him she had another surprise for him. The look on his face warned her that he hadn't been too crazy about the first one.

"We're going on a trip," she told him, pretending an excitement she couldn't really feel. "We're going away together, just you and me. So pack your things, sweetie."

"A trip?" Robbie's eyes were very big. "Where to?"

She hesitated. "I'm not sure about that just yet. We'll go where the mood takes us. Okay?"

He nodded, though she was sure he had very little idea what she meant by that.

"So you'd better go in and start deciding what you want to take. One bag of toys, one bag of clothes. Okay?"

"Okay," he said and started to leave the room. But he stopped halfway to the door and turned slowly back. "Is that guy gone?" he asked her.

Charlie stopped what she was doing, her heart in her throat for some reason. "What guy?"

"That Denver guy. Is he gone for good?"

Charlie looked at her son, searched his dear round face. "Yes," she said quietly. "I think he is."

Robbie's face cleared and he looked happy. "Good."

"Didn't you like him?" Charlie asked.

Robbie shook his head.

"Then maybe," she murmured to herself, "it's just as well he's gone."

Just as well, just as well. The phrase rolled around in her mind as she worked. It was just as well that things had turned out as they had. Wasn't it? Having Denver around was bad enough, but playing house would have been devastating. With sudden, sure conviction, she knew what would have happened if he'd agreed to be her pretend husband. The thought of his arms around her again made something fall away in the bottom of her stomach. That darn man had opened her eyes to possibilities she'd just as soon be blind to.

"This is a real bummer," she muttered as she began to throw clothes into her suitcase. Why had Denver ever come into her life? She'd been doing just fine without him and he certainly hadn't done her any good. He'd awakened feelings she'd forgotten existed, feelings she'd managed to push down into the dark corners of her being, feelings she'd assumed had just about died away from neglect after all this time.

He'd awakened her hunger. The word shocked her and she stopped with an old patched pair of jeans in her hand, staring through the glass at the mountains. She might as well call it what it was. Hunger, a deep, aching need for a man. He'd reached down inside and found it in her, coaxed it out, and now she was going to have to deal with the thing until she could get it tamed and back in its hiding place again. And she had a feeling that was going to take a long time.

"Thanks, Denver," she said, shaking out the jeans and throwing them in the bag for charity. "Thanks a lot."

Eight

Denver was having a hard time getting the feel of Charlie out of his mind. Something about her clung to his senses and wouldn't leave him alone. He'd come up here to the mountains for rest and relaxation, but instead he'd found a way to build up more stress.

How did you lose the memory of a woman, anyway? He wasn't sure. He hadn't really had to deal with this sort of thing before. Most of his relations with the softer sex had been mutually short-term and superficial. Out of sight, out of mind. That was the way he'd always dealt with women. The one exception, the one time he'd fallen in love, had been different, but he'd been so young and naive at the time, the comparison hardly applied here. Besides, when it was over, it was over. He hadn't looked back much.

But this damn thing with Charlie wasn't over that way because it had never started. Not really. That was the problem. It wasn't really anything you could name. It hung around like…like…

"Like a cloud of mosquitoes," he muttered to himself as he gazed out at a circling hawk.

Yeah, that was a good representation of it. Annoying. Unpleasant. All potential bite, no staying power.

And just as he was congratulating himself for that unpleasant mind picture, he caught the scent of honeysuckle in the air and the memory of the smell of her filled his head, tightening his body like a drum.

He groaned. This was no good. He had to get out of here, do something, get his mind on something else. Fishing. That would do the trick. He'd go into the little town and buy some fishing supplies.

His leg was feeling a lot better today, almost normal. He hiked down pretty easily to where his car was parked, and drove along the dusty road, passing the ski lift with the lines hanging limply and the sign that offered a quick sale for the right price. Further down the hill he came to a liquor store in an A-frame, then the little restaurant where Charlie said she worked, and just across the street was the general store he'd noticed on the way in the day before. Built originally as a log cabin, it had sustained extension after extension through the years, but it still retained its rustic charm. A beautiful old woodstove sat in the corner, all gleaming stainless steel, and pieces of timber with notches carved out of them to resemble the heads of wolves and deer sat around on counters. There was a bait basin full of something wiggling and a display of lures and colorful flies. Engaged in looking all these things over, Denver didn't notice the conversation going on in the front of the store at first. When he did, he stopped to listen.

"Look, mister," the rather jovial man behind the counter was saying. "If she was here, someone would have recognized her by now."

"You know," the man he was talking to replied, "that's just what I thought at first. Seems a little strange that no one has come forward, doesn't it?"

Denver tensed. All he could see was the back of the man's head, but he knew that voice.

"Listen," the storekeeper said, losing patience. "I put the picture up, just like you asked me. I can't help it if no one around here has ever seen the girl. If you can find her here, more power to you. But if not, I'm afraid that's just your problem."

The stranger seemed to be having a bad day and his annoyance with the world and all who inhabited it was clear in his tone. "I'm going to find her if I have to dredge the lakes."

The local man reacted to that. "Dredge the lakes? Are you crazy?"

"You never know," the stranger continued, smugly. "Her family is concerned she might be suicidal. Wouldn't that be a nice bit of publicity for your resort area?"

The local man seemed to grow in stature, fueled by a building anger. "Mister, you better not be threatening me...."

But the stranger put up a hand and shook his head. "Now, now, no need to get testy. I've got a few leads. I got a nice tip last night. Someone told me she might be working in one of the restaurants in the evening. I'm going to check that out, and if that doesn't pan out—well, I'll just have to go on to the next phase."

He pushed away from the counter. "Listen, let me know if you hear anything from anyone. Someone's got to know where she is. And just give me a call. The number's on the back of the photo.''

The visitor turned and began to make his way out of the building, and Denver drew back into another aisle so that they wouldn't come face-to-face. He not only knew the voice, he knew the man.

''Mark Harris,'' he murmured softly, confirming his identification by looking out the window and watching the man get into his car.

He'd known Mark Harris for years, more by reputation than in a personal way. As a private investigator, he worked out of Los Angeles, usually covering the west side, finding runaway rich kids for their wealthy parents and cleaning up the messes they made on their journeys. Denver had come in contact with his work in relation to a few cases he was working on himself. ''So that's who Mrs. Chandler sends to find her daughter.''

Denver made his way to the counter. The local man was ringing up bubble gum for a couple of kids. Finishing that, he turned to Denver.

''What can I do you for?'' he asked, cheerful now that the private detective was gone.

Denver's gaze flashed around the counter and then his eyes narrowed. ''Something tells me I could get a hand-rolled Cuban if I played my cards just right,'' he said softly.

The man gave him a sharp look, then glanced around the store and relaxed. ''Now, how did you know that?'' he answered, also speaking low. ''It just so happens I might be able to get you in touch with one. For a price.'' He named an exorbitant sum, enough to keep a family of four happy on a long weekend, but Denver didn't blink. Quickly and discreetly, they made the first half of their exchange, money for the illegally imported cigar, and the man headed for a back room, just as Denver had hoped he would have to do.

Waiting until the man was out of sight, Denver moved with quiet confidence to the end of the counter and reached across it, snagging the picture propped there between two fingers and dropping it slickly in the pocket of his jacket without anyone else in the store noticing a thing. He was back in position when the man reentered the room. Thanking him for the cigar, he left the place. He hesitated as he passed a trash can. Smoking didn't happen to be a vice of his. But somehow, having paid that much, he couldn't just throw the thing away. Thrusting it into his other pocket, he decided to save it for his boss. Josh Hoya loved a good cigar. Boy, was he going to be pleased with this one.

Once out of the storekeeper's line of vision, he pulled the picture out of his pocket and held it up where he could get a good look at it. Just as he'd suspected, it was Charlie. He looked around quickly at the people entering the store. There must be a constant stream of locals in and out. Why didn't everyone immediately see the resemblance? This was Charlie. Or rather, Adrianna Charlyne Chandler the third. Didn't they see it?

Looking back at the picture, he began to see why it might be that most people would miss the resemblance. The face was young, rounded, and the hair was cropped close to the head in a gamine cut. But what was most different were the eyes. There was a sad and haunted look to the eyes that wasn't there now. Whatever problems she might be having, Charlie was basically a happy woman these days. In the picture, she was anything but.

He tried to remember back to when he'd seen her at the school with his sister. She hadn't seemed unhappy to him then. But that was something he might not have noticed in those days. All he knew was that she was rich, pampered, a symbol of everything he'd wanted for his sister, and yet somehow so far out of reach…

But he had to think this through. Mark Harris was an idiot, but he wasn't half bad as an investigator. His reputation was well known and not too clean. He usually got what he went after and he didn't always use ethical means to do it. There was no way he could in good conscience leave Charlie unprotected with Mark Harris after her.

But wait a minute. He had to let her be. If he hung around, he was going to fall for her. He could feel it coming, like the swell before a wave formed in the ocean. He had to nip this thing in the bud. Maybe…maybe he could warn her first. Let her know what was coming down the pike. But he couldn't do more than that.

Charlie. He looked at the picture again, looked at those sad eyes. That same woman had been in his arms the night before and she'd been as warm and open as any woman he'd ever been with. What had happened to her? What had happened between those schooldays and these? What had changed her?

He stood in the street, undecided, fishing tackle in one hand, her picture in the other. He'd come up here for rest and relaxation. Long, lazy days of fishing had been in his mind. And now, this.

Two boys were passing him. He looked up in time

to see the elbow of one hit the ribs of the other, and then he heard the first boy hiss, "Look. It's Robbie Smith's dad."

Both pair of eyes were fixed on him as the boys passed. He let them go without a correction and something inside him stirred uncomfortably. Robbie's dad. Who was spreading that kind of rumor? He looked back into the glass of the general store, staring at his own reflection. Was that really what people thought Robbie's dad ought to look like?

Robbie's dad. He groaned and let his head fall back. The sky was china blue and cloudless. "Oh, what the hell," he muttered, straightening. He set his shoulders and turned toward the Pali, across the street. He might as well face it. Rest and relaxation were out the window and it was time for him to get back to doing what he'd been trained in all his life—finding out the truth about what was going on.

Charlie was dragging her heavy suitcase out onto the porch and wondering how she was going to tie it to the back of the scooter when Denver came driving up in front of her house. She stood very still, watching him slowly get out of his car. The sunlight gleamed on his hair and flashed in his eyes, and she melted inside. There was no other way to describe it.

His gaze held hers as he came toward her and her heart was thumping in her throat. "Put that thing back," he told her coolly, gesturing toward the suitcase. "Have you got a good-sized backpack?"

She nodded. She hadn't said a word of greeting to him yet. She was waiting, every nerve quivering, to find out what he was doing here.

"Good," he said. "Put some things in it and let's

get out of here." He jerked his head toward the mountains. "Why don't you show me some countryside?"

She stood staring at him. This was the same man who had said he couldn't pretend to be her husband, even for a day or two. Now he wanted to go hiking? "What are you talking about?" she asked at last.

"You and me." He shrugged his wide shoulders. "Let's go backpacking for a couple of days. Get out of here. Breathe some fresh air."

Her confusion was clear on her face. "But…"

"Get someone to take care of Robbie," he said, anticipating her first objection.

Quickly, she shook her head. "No," she said firmly, breathless but sure of this at least. "Robbie goes with me."

He hesitated. He would rather not take the kid along. Kids were always trouble. Besides, he would surely slow them down. But he could see he was outvoted by the stubborn look in her eyes, and he nodded curtly. "Okay. Get him packed up, too. But let's get out of here within the hour."

She stared at him, not moving, but not completely under his spell as yet. "Listen," she said quietly. "You show up here out of the blue and order me to go off into the hills with you. I don't understand. Why? And most of all, why should I trust you?"

He pulled the picture out of his pocket and showed it to her. "I found this being displayed at the general store. This is you, isn't it?"

Her eyes widened and she nodded, her voice suddenly stuck in her throat. The instinct to turn and run was strong, but where would she run to? She stayed where she was and waited, breathing hard.

"You were right about someone being after you,"

he said, dropping the picture back into his pocket. "I know the guy. He's good. He's going to find you. Unless I help you."

She glanced quickly at his car, but he read her mind.

"Heading out on wheels isn't going to do it. He'll be watching for that, and he'll have contacts in every town around here. Once he's got the scent up the way he does, he won't let you slip past him."

She looked at him, feeling helpless, feeling as though he—tall, strong, with shoulders that filled the horizon—as though he were her only hope. "Then what can I do?" she asked him.

"Head into the hills. After a few days, he'll think you got by him somehow and he'll go on to the next good prospect. That won't fix things for good, but it'll give you a window of time to decide what to do next."

She frowned, searching his face, the suitcase forgotten on the wooden floor of the porch. He seemed to loom larger all the time, taller, harder, stronger. Should she trust him?

She didn't know, but that didn't stop her from asking him, "Do you really think so?" as though he knew everything. And for all she knew, maybe he did.

He nodded in answer to her question. "I know the man. I know his modus operandi. Trust me."

He said it as though it would be a simple thing, an easy thing, a thing that followed naturally.

"Trust me." Easy to say the words. Hard to do what the words implied. She stared at him. She knew there wasn't much time. "Trust me," he was saying. The only man she'd ever put her complete naive trust in was Jeff, and he'd betrayed her almost immediately. She'd been pretty sure she would never really trust a man again. And yet, there he was, so strong and con-

fident, so sure that she would, and should, trust him
with her life, with her son's life.

She began to walk toward him as though compelled.
As she reached where he was standing, she put her
hand out and took hold of the front of his jacket, pulling him closer. Her head tilted back, she stared straight
into his face.

"Kiss me," she demanded, her eyes bright as the
sun. "Kiss me quick and hard. Do it now."

He didn't hesitate. His mouth on hers was hot as
fire, burning her like a brand. "Okay," she said, pulling away again with a gasp. "I'll go get us ready."

He watched her disappear into her house and he
wiped his mouth with the back of his hand, wishing
he could erase what had just happened. She'd demanded the kiss and he hadn't wavered. Hell, he'd
wanted to do it, wanted to do a whole lot more. There
was no doubt about that. But it hadn't been the right
thing to do, even if she did need it to reassure her that
he was for real.

"No more kissing," he vowed to himself. "That's
not what this is all about."

But he knew he was lying to himself. That *was* what
this was about, and he knew he was going to have to
get used to it.

Nine

___

The mountains still had at least four hours of daylight left when Denver, Charlie and Robbie finally started out. They rode in Denver's car to the trailhead, then set out on foot, following a wilderness trail that would take them to crystal-clear high mountain lakes and frosty tumbling streams threaded between stands of shimmering aspen and gnarled bristlecone pine.

"Are you sure we know what we're doing?" Charlie had asked Denver as they packed the car. "Where exactly are we going?"

"Out of our minds," would have been an answer that wouldn't have surprised her, but that wasn't the answer he gave.

"Don't worry," he told her, glancing at her sideways. "I've talked to some people. I've got a destination in mind."

"But you're not going to share?" she asked in wonder.

His quick grin reassured her. "You'll find out soon enough. But if you really want to know, here." He pulled a piece of paper with a crude map drawn on it out of his pocket. "You can take a look. We should make it by tomorrow afternoon. About ten hours' hiking should do it."

"But your knee," Charlie protested, spreading the map out and realizing she hadn't a clue as to what it all meant. "How will you be able to take all that climbing?"

"I've got it tightly wrapped," he told her. "Don't worry about me. I'll let you know when I need to stop." He traced the trail along the map with his forefinger. "It looks like an easy hike, not much altitude until along about here." He pointed it out on the paper, checking the height markings. "I've done worse."

She tilted her head back and looked up at him. "You always say that," she noted. "Someday you're going to have to tell me all about your wild adventures."

He looked down into her eyes in surprise, and the look between the two of them seemed to acknowledge that there was going to be a "someday" in their relationship. They were more than mere acquaintances now. They were even more than casual friends. He didn't know what they were going to end up being, and he didn't want to know. But he knew it was going to be something like he'd never had before.

Their hour had turned into almost two by the time they were ready to go. Charlie had called Ernie and negotiated some time off after all. He'd been so quick to give the leave to her, she'd almost been suspicious. But what could there possibly be behind his offer but his usual kindness?

They'd packed enough food for two days. They hadn't had time to get proper hiking supplies, so their stash was rather amateurish.

"Bring along some cans of beef stew," he'd told her when she'd asked what he wanted. "That always tastes real good in the wilderness."

Beef stew. Pretty close to pot roast, she thought at the time. Denver is a meat and potatoes sort of guy, all right.

She hadn't told anyone else they were going. She hadn't even talked to Denver much. She had no idea how long he planned for them to stay in the mountains or what they would do next. They were going, that was all. As soon as the decision had been made, she'd felt such a sense of relief, she could hardly wait to get there. She wanted to walk very fast, to leave the problem behind, to be in the cool air, as far away from people as she could get. Once she got very far away, she would have the space to think through what her next step should be, where she would go from here.

And so their little party was off, striding down the trail, passing the reservoir and heading into the lonely back country. Though this was supposed to be Charlie's territory, Denver knew she wasn't a real mountaineer and that he was going to have to take charge of what they did and how they did it. That was fine with him. He liked to be sure of where things were going. He hadn't put in so many successful years doing the sort of work he did by letting other people cover for him.

He glanced back. Robbie was clomping along be-

hind him, looking like a miniature adult in his big
hiking boots with his pack on his back. Sabrina had a
pack tied to her back, too, and a red kerchief around
her neck, and she was trotting along beside the boy,
looking more subdued than Denver would have expected. And Charlie was bringing up the back of the
parade, keeping an eye on her son, making sure everything was going along all right. Denver gave her a
nod and she smiled at him, and there was something
in that smile that made it so his knee didn't feel bad
at all. He took a deep breath and wondered why this
felt so good—to be heading out into nowhere with
Charlie. Maybe he was just being a fool. But if he
was, he had to admit, he sort of liked it.

Charlie didn't know the extent of his feelings, but
she could sense at least some of them. There was
something growing between them. She should have
been scared of it, but she wasn't. Not yet. She was
enjoying it for the moment. Still, she didn't know why
he was doing this. She just thanked the stars that he
was.

She'd never considered heading into the mountains
before. Living on beans and trout in the wild wasn't
really a part of her background, even though she'd
called this area her home for six years. When Denver
had brought it up, she'd been stunned by the brilliance
of his idea. The mountains. Of course. All good fu-
gitives hid out in the mountains, didn't they?

Robbie had balked a bit at first—not about their
destination—that thrilled him. But he did take exception to their company.

"You said he was gone for good," he complained
when he heard what they were going to do.

"I was wrong. He came back."

Robbie threw himself face-down on his bed and kicked his feet in the air. ''Why does he have to come with us?''

She dropped to sit beside him on the bed, running her fingers through his featherlight hair. ''Don't you like him?''

He shook his head stubbornly and she'd begun making faces, always a surefire way to tease him out of his pouty face. He worked very hard not to laugh, but when she crossed her eyes, he couldn't help it. All he let go was one quick blast of laughter, though. And then he was stone-faced again.

Charlie sighed and gave up. ''He's a friend, Robbie. You don't have to do anything special with him. But you do have to be polite. I won't stand for any rudeness. You hear?''

He'd heard, and though he'd looked sulky at first, once they were a few minutes down the trail he'd forgotten all about being mad in the excitement.

''Are we gonna see a bear?'' he asked Denver, his blue eyes round as marbles.

''Not if he sees us first,'' Denver had joked.

And Robbie had laughed for a second before he'd remembered that he didn't like Denver, and sobered quickly. But Denver had stopped him and showed him how to wear his pack so that it didn't cut into his shoulders and the sulky look had disappeared for good then.

For a time, he walked up next to Denver, and after a few minutes of doing that, he glanced up at the tall man and decided to start a small conversation.

''Hey, Denver,'' he said, taking three steps with his short legs to every one the man took. ''Do you have a gun?''

Denver gazed at him ruefully. "Why do you want to know? Does Billy's dad have a gun?"

Robbie nodded. "Uh-huh."

Denver's mouth twisted and his eyes sparkled. "What a surprise."

"He's a cop," Robbie said.

"Oh." Denver nodded.

Robbie looked up at him again, his blue eyes bright with interest. "Are you a cop?"

He hesitated. "Not exactly."

"I'm going to learn to shoot a gun," Robbie said happily, giving a skip to show his excitement. "Since we're going to live in the woods, I have to."

Denver laughed softly, too softly for the boy to tell. "Does your mother know about this plan yet?" he asked him.

Robbie shook his head candidly. "No. *I'm* not going to tell her."

"I think you'd better tell her," Denver advised him.

Robbie scrunched up his face and looked at Denver. "'Cuz she's my mom?"

"Yup."

Robbie sighed. "Okay. I will." He looked up at the large man beside him. "Did you have a mom?"

Denver nodded. "We all have them," he told the boy solemnly.

Robbie thought for a moment. "But not dads," he said at last. He made a singsong out of it. "No dads, some people got no dads." And then he ran back to find Sabrina.

It wasn't long before Robbie and the dog were running on ahead, the two of them dashing along the dusty trail as though they could hardly wait to see what was over the next ridge.

"They make quite a pair, don't they?" Denver said, grinning as he watched them run, the boy with his stubby, sturdy little legs, the dog with her reddish fur flying and her tongue lolling.

"Oh yes," Charlie told him. "It's as though they have their own language between the two of them."

"Do you ever feel left out?" he asked her, glancing at her sideways and enjoying the way the sunlight lit her face.

"Me? Oh no." She laughed at the thought. "I love it when he's happy."

He shifted the weight in his pack and asked, without looking at her, "How about you, Charlie? What makes you happy?"

She paused. There were a lot of new things she might have told him about, new things she hadn't been aware of until the last twenty-four hours. But she let that go, and went back to her standby. "Robbie makes me happy," she said stoutly. "He's my masterpiece." She flashed him a quick look. "I don't need anything else," she added, lying through her teeth.

"Don't you?" He looked down and met her gaze and she was sure he saw it all in her eyes—the new awareness, the new need—the fact that she was very much afraid that she was falling in love with him.

But if he saw all that, he made no sign. He smiled and made a joke that she couldn't really hear because of the buzzing in her ears, and then he pointed out an eagle's nest and the moment passed.

But she knew something now she hadn't known before. They were going to make love. Sooner or later, it was going to happen. And much as she was falling for him, that scared her. She remembered lovemaking with Jeff. Gross and awkward were the words that came to mind. She didn't want to have that happen between her and Denver. But she knew she was going to risk it anyway. It was something that had to be.

Robbie and Sabrina made a lot of noise ahead, and then, as they entered an area where the ground was rough with shale and began to slope steeply downward, they ran further ahead and Charlie began to frown. "Robbie, wait!" she called out, but Denver stopped her with a hand on her arm.

"Let him go," he told her. "He's a kid. He's got to try his wings a little."

She looked up at him in astonishment. "Oh, really? And where do you come by this advanced knowledge of child-rearing?" she asked him, almost resentful.

He shrugged. "I don't know," he answered honestly, a little surprised himself. "I just know it, that's all." On second thought, maybe he did know how that could be. "I was a kid myself once, you know," he reminded her.

She put a hand up to shade her eyes and followed the path Robbie and Sabrina were blazing, walking a little faster so as to keep up with them. "But there could be rattlers," she said worriedly. "Or coyotes. Or mountain lions."

"Or he could fall and skin his knee and learn not to run so fast downhill again," he told her sensibly. "Look, it's not like we're sending him on ahead out of sight. I've got my eye on him. But you've got to let him make his own mistakes."

She bit her lip. "As long as they aren't lethal mistakes," she muttered.

"Of course," he told her. "That's what we're here to make sure of."

She wasn't completely sure he was right. After all,

she'd been the boy's mother for a long time and things had worked out pretty well the way she'd done them so far. But Robbie was a boy, and there were times she'd wished she had a man around just to help her understand what made boys the way they were. So she let it go for now.

Denver's knee lasted almost two hours into the hike, and then he had to surrender to pain and take a rest. He found a place near the edge of the stream, a flat, grassy area under the shade of a tall old redwood, and he lowered himself painfully to the ground and closed his eyes.

"This is no good at all," Charlie fretted, dropping her pack and sitting down on the ground beside him. "You're going to do permanent damage to that knee if you don't take it easy." She glanced around the clearing. "We could just stay here," she suggested. "No one is going to come this far in to look for us."

Opening his eyes, he looked at her and smiled. "No dice, Charlie. Just as soon as I get my strength back, we're moving on. We've got a destination, you know."

She gazed at him speculatively. "So you said before. But you haven't told me where it is. You really haven't told me anything at all."

He nodded. "It's better that way. You wait and see."

She sighed with exasperation, but she didn't dwell on it. She started talking about something else right away. He looked up at her. She didn't seem to care very much, as though she was more concerned with the journey than with the end of it. She was commenting on the trees and the sound of the wind in the treetops mixed with the sound of the water in the stream and how wonderful it was to breathe this fresh air. The late-afternoon sun filled her face with light and shadows and the breeze played with the free strands of her hair. She was the most beautiful woman he'd ever seen. She always had been, but now there was more to it than he'd known before. There was a core of goodness to her, a worth and a value that shone through the beauty, making it all the more precious.

He stopped himself, appalled. What the hell was the matter with him? He never did this sort of thing. He never thought this way. If he didn't watch out, he'd go falling in love or something equally silly and dangerous. And he couldn't let that happen.

She seemed to sense the change in his mood, and she turned toward him, frowning. "Why did you decide to do this?" she asked him suddenly. "Why did you change your mind?"

He looked out toward the river. This wasn't something he wanted to talk about. Or even think about. Still, the woman wanted to talk, and he was stuck here like a staked tiger. He stirred restlessly. From the noise they were making, he could tell that Robbie and Sabrina were occupied down along the banks of the stream, far enough away so that he could talk privately with Charlie and not worry about Robbie hearing him. He could say anything he wanted. Still, he hesitated.

"Does it have something to do with Gail?" she said, pulling the band out of her hair and letting the strands fly free in the breeze.

"Gail?" he repeated, surprised. "What do you mean?"

"I got the impression you two were estranged in some way," she said, combing her fingers through her hair, taking out the snarls. "I remember how you al-

ways used to take care of her." She smiled at him
with a quick and easy affection that tore a hole in his
heart. "You were the most loving brother..."

He shook his head. "I don't want to talk about
Gail," he said evenly.

She leaned over him, looking down, her hair flying
around them both. "I thought maybe you were trying
to prove something. Make amends, maybe, by taking
care of me..."

He pulled himself up so that they were face-to-face.
"That's crazy," he said, avoiding her gaze by looking
at her mouth. "Don't try to psychoanalyze me, Charlie. It won't work."

"Oh, no?" She was half teasing him now. "You
mean you might turn out to be a good guy after all?"

He stared at her for a long moment, then rose to
stand. She rose along with him, staying close, closer
than she normally might have. He could feel the heat
coming from her body, feel it as though he could see
it, as though he could reach out and touch it. "Don't
make me out to be something I'm not, Charlie," he
warned her at last. "I'm no saint."

"No?" She gazed at him for a moment, then surprised him by reaching up to touch his cheek with her
finger for a fleeting moment. "What are you, then?"

She was too close, too tempting, too soft and round
and blond. Didn't she realize what she was asking for,
acting like this? He wasn't sure she did, and he knew
someone ought to warn her. Maybe he ought to warn
her himself.

Moving on reflex, he grabbed her by the hair at the
back of her head and forced her face an inch from his
own. "I'm probably harder and rougher and less refined than any man you've ever been with, Charlie,"

he told her, his voice a low rumble in his throat. "Don't take this lightly." In some confused part of his brain the move had been meant to scare her off, make her think twice about getting involved with him, but he saw the flare at the back of her eyes, felt the tingle on her skin, and he knew it hadn't worked that way.

"I take you very seriously," she told him softly, her voice pulsing with the excitement he was rousing in her blood. "You are the most serious thing that has happened to me since—"

He didn't know why he wanted to stop her, stop the words coming from her mouth, but he did. And the only way he could find was to kiss her. His mouth took hers, though he wasn't sure if she would want him, and she moved nearer to take him in and hold him close, and something passed between them that was electric, that made them both shiver. And the shiver quickly became a throb and his arms tightened around her, and he pulled her hard up against him so that she could feel how much he wanted her, so that she would know where they were going, that this wasn't just a game. And Charlie gasped and pulled her head away.

"No," she whispered, glancing over his shoulder at the stream where Robbie was playing. "We can't forget Robbie." She began to slip out of his arms.

"Hey, Denver," Robbie called at that very moment, his head appearing from behind a ragweed bush. "Come here, quick. I found some baby frogs!"

Denver looked at Charlie but she avoided meeting his gaze, and he took a deep breath and got up, going to see the baby frogs. He stayed to talk to Robbie, but he glanced back frequently at where Charlie sat very still, as though listening to the wind again.

They should have a talk about the kissing, he decided as they started back along the trail. And the touching. If they didn't, it would just happen again. Then he stopped himself and laughed softly. Hell, it was going to happen again no matter what he did, and he knew it. In fact, the anticipation was burning in his blood, beating in his veins. It was going to take more than talking to stop this juggernaut that was building in his body...and in hers.

He should go off and leave them. He should have sent them on their way and waved goodbye. He should have got in his car, left the town and driven like a bat out of hell for the city. He should have called headquarters for a new assignment, something really hazardous that would have engaged his mind, just to keep her out of it. But he hadn't and he wouldn't. What would be would be.

And maybe that was for the best. Maybe...maybe if he took her, if he had her for his own for one night, if he solved the mystery in her eyes and conquered his fears and her doubts, maybe he would be able to free himself from the fascination that had haunted him for so long.

Maybe. And then again, maybe not.

The wind became chilly as soon as the sun disappeared behind the mountains. There was still plenty of light, but the temperature was going down fast and they were getting tired.

"I'll tell you one thing," Charlie told him as they marched along side by side. "We're having beef stew tonight. I want to get rid of a couple of these cans. They get awfully heavy.''

It was only a few minutes later that they found a good place to camp for the night. There didn't seem to be much point in going on. Charlie found herself humming as she washed her face and hands in the stream and she stopped in disbelief. What right did she have to be happy, anyway? She was on the run, leaving behind responsibilities and friends, taking her son away from school and everything he'd always known, throwing him in with a man who didn't even like kids.

Well, she had to amend that one. He'd been showing a willingness to change that point of view. She didn't know if he was doing it just to make her happy or if he really was beginning to like Robbie, and really, she supposed it didn't matter at this point. The important thing was, he was treating her son with kindness and that was all she asked.

''I know you don't want to talk about it,'' she'd said to him a short time ago on the trail. ''But I think it's only fair if you let me know what has happened to Gail. I haven't heard from her for…well, since I left home. If something has happened to her…I care about her and I really want to know.''

He didn't answer for so long, she thought maybe he wasn't going to answer. But just before she prodded him again, he grimaced and began.

''She's not sick or dead or anything like that,'' he'd told her curtly. ''She made some choices I couldn't agree with. She went off to live a life I couldn't accept. And I don't want to talk about it.''

That brought all sorts of ideas into her head. What could Gail have done to break the tie she'd had with her brother? Charlie remembered very well how close they'd been, how Gail had always run to phone her brother whenever she had good news. Gail had been a sweet, good-natured girl, full of fun, but always worried about what her brother might think. It was hard to imagine what might have caused the rift between them.

Charlie sat back on her heels and frowned, wondering, but the sound of Robbie and Sabrina arriving, shoes and paws clattering against the rocks, turned her head and her thoughts and she smiled at her boy and patted the dog's head.

"Guess what?" Robbie announced proudly. "Denver is going to teach me how to make a fire."

His eyes were so bright, it made her smile, but she pretended to be unimpressed. "Oh, pshaw. I can teach you that. You just take out a book of matches…"

"No, Mommy." His face was a mirror of distaste. "Not like that. Like Indians do. With sticks."

"Oh. I see. Modern conveniences aren't good enough for the two of you, huh?"

Robbie rolled his big blue eyes. "Mommy! You gotta make a fire the right way. 'Case you ever get lost in the woods."

"Of course," she said, laughing as she rose and turned back toward where Denver was preparing the camp. "How silly of me to forget about that."

Denver impressed her with his patience as he taught Robbie how to rub sticks together and maybe get a puff of smoke if you were lucky. And they were only a little lucky. They finally resorted to the matches and Charlie tried not to gloat, but the teasing went back and forth both ways, and they were all laughing as they sat back to eat the beef stew and corn bread she'd warmed for them. Even Sabrina looked as though she'd got the jokes; sitting beside Robbie with her tongue lolling, she seemed to be laughing, too. The feeling was wonderful and warm and Charlie held it inside and cherished it.

At the same time, Denver was noticing that Robbie was covertly staring at him. He caught him doing it three times in about four minutes, and he began to feel hemmed in, just a little annoyed. Why the heck wasn't the kid paying less attention to him and more attention to his food? But then he noticed what the boy was doing, how he was holding his fork, the way he was smiling into the fire, and realization hit him. The kid was copying him. The kid was trying to pattern everything he did after what he'd seen Denver do. Suddenly he saw it in a whole new light. He'd never thought of himself as a role model before. But now he was beginning to understand what that meant. There was a whole new level of responsibility that went with it. He had to be careful of what he said and what he did. He couldn't risk teaching Robbie something wrong. This was serious. He couldn't help it. He felt proud.

Charlie watched the interplay between the two of them and hid a smile. Denver was warming to Robbie. She could see it and she was glad. If she was going to fall in love with the man, it would help if he liked her child.

A little later, while she was cleaning the dishes by the stream, Robbie left Denver by the campfire and came out to join her. She handed him a dish to dry and showed him where to put it on the flat rock she'd designated for that purpose. And then he floored her with a question she hadn't expected.

"Mommy?" he said softly, forgetting to dry and holding the plate motionless in front of him. "Is Denver my real dad?"

Charlie dropped the pot she'd been holding on the ground, glad it was aluminum, and turned to her boy, taking both his shoulders in her hands so that she could see his face.

"Oh, Robbie, no," she said, trying to keep her emotions in check so that he wouldn't hear them in her voice. "Where did you ever get such an idea?"

His big blue eyes flashed in the moonlight. "Yesterday when you came to get me at school and you said you had a surprise for me. I thought maybe you got me what I wanted for my birthday."

Her hands slid to his back and she pulled him close for a hug. "You never told me you wanted a dad for your birthday," she said sadly, rocking him.

"But I did want one."

"But, Robbie…" She pulled back so that she could look into his face again.

"Then I saw Denver," he went on innocently, "and I thought, 'Maybe he's my dad,' but he said he didn't have any little boys. And he didn't like me. So I knew he wasn't my dad."

Charlie gasped. "Robbie, he likes you very much. He just wasn't used to kids. He didn't know how to talk to you. He's getting better all the time. Can't you tell?"

Robbie looked at her, his eyes scrunched and his nose wrinkled. "Then, could he be my dad?"

She shook her head. "Robbie, I told you what happened to your dad. He died before you were born."

He bit his lip and hung his head. "He can't come back, huh?"

Her hands cupped his shoulders lovingly. "No, Robbie. He can't come back."

Robbie looked at her with a very serious and sad little face. "So I never get a dad? Not ever?"

"Robbie, darling…" Her voice choked with tears and she didn't know what to say to him. She couldn't promise him a dad. But she couldn't act as though his request meant nothing, as though the two of them should be happy to be alone together for the rest of time. She'd never understood before just how deep and pure the need for a father was in a child. And she'd never felt so inadequate at reassuring him.

"Charlie."

At the sound of his voice, she turned with a start. Denver stood in the clearing just behind them. How much had he heard? Enough, evidently. He had a look on his face she'd never seen there before.

"Charlie, let me talk to Robbie," he said softly. "Alone."

She turned and looked at her boy. He looked apprehensive, but very brave.

"Why?" she asked, hesitating. This was her boy. She was the only one who had ever ministered to his fears. Why should she give way to this man who hardly knew him?

"I've got a secret to tell him about," Denver said, and she looked at him, incredulous.

"What are you talking about?"

He looked at her hard for a moment, then took her hand in his and raised it to his lips, planting a kiss in the middle of her palm. "Don't worry," he told her softly, his eyes luminous. "I'm not going to hurt him."

Her fingers curled around his hand, as though she

could force him to do the right thing somehow. "Words can hurt," she warned him, unconvinced.

"I know that. Trust me."

Their gazes held for a long moment. She tried to read his mind. Robbie was the most precious thing on earth to her. If she trusted Denver with her son, did that mean she trusted him with everything? Like maybe, her heart?

But that wasn't the issue here. Her son and his fears were the important thing. If Denver could help with that, she would just have another reason to love him. She remembered the kiss. She didn't know why that meant everything to her, but it did.

"All right," she said, her voice shaking. "I'll just go and get our bedrolls ready for the night."

Denver nodded, waiting for her to leave. She left briskly. Once a decision had been made, she liked to get it over with. He watched her go, then slowly, wincing a little, he lowered himself to sit on a log beside the boy.

"Robbie," he told him casually. "I heard some of the things you were saying to your mom, and it made me think that it's probably time I told you about the Secret Dad's Club. Have you ever heard of it before?"

"The Secret Dad's Club?" Robbie repeated it as though he liked the words. He readjusted the way he was sitting so that he would be an exact replica of the man beside him. "No. I never did."

Denver nodded. "Well, club members don't talk about it much. Not to the rest of the world, anyway. Only to kids who need them."

Robbie's eyes widened and he kicked his heels in the sand. "What kinds of kids?"

"Kids like you. Kids who don't have a dad around at the time."

Robbie's mouth dropped and he looked at Denver in wonder. "There's a club about it?" he asked, his voice higher than usual.

Denver smiled at him. "Sure. All the dads in the world belong to it. And even some guys like me who don't have any kids. Yet," he added quickly. "See, if you belong to the club, every time you see a kid who doesn't have a dad at home, you're supposed to help be a secret dad to him."

"Really?" There was a sense of wonder in his voice that made Denver grin.

"Sure. To be a secret dad to him...or her," he amended. "This goes for girls, too. They need dads. Did you know that?"

Robbie shook his head, deeply interested. "I didn't know that," he said solemnly.

"They do. Anyway, the members are out there all the time. Every time a man is nice to you, or does something that a dad might do, you'll know. He's a member."

Robbie cocked his head to the side, wondering. "What do they do?"

Denver shrugged. "Well, if you had a dad, what would he do with you?"

Robbie thought for a moment. "He would go hiking with me," he said, "and tell me how to do things. And play ball. And maybe he would..." He frowned hard, trying to think of something else.

"Wrestle a gorilla?" Denver offered.

Robbie shook his head as though to shake that thought away. "Naw," he said. "I know that didn't happen."

"Good. Because that's not part of what the secret dads do."

Robbie nodded, his shiny hair bouncing on his round little head. "Maybe he would teach me how to shoot," he said hopefully, glancing sideways at Denver.

Denver chuckled. "Only if he was brave enough to face your mother," he said.

But Robbie was undeterred. "Sure," he answered. "He'd be that brave. Wouldn't he?"

Denver shook his head. "I don't know. But you do understand about this, don't you? The members aren't real dads to the kids. They can't be around all the time. But when they can, they will step in and be a dad. What do you think? Do you like it?"

Robbie thought for a minute, scrunching his face into a mass of difficult assessment. "I think so," he said doubtfully. "We could try it."

"Great." Denver held out his hand and took Robbie's little paw into it, shaking firmly. "It's a deal." He rose. "Now let's go help your mother with the bedrolls."

The boy jumped up and ran toward the camp. Denver followed more slowly, and when that annoying voice inside his head began to chide him for getting too close to Robbie, he brushed it away. "There are some things," he told it evenly, "more important than keeping safe. And taking care of a young boy like that is one of them."

To his surprise, the voice shut up and didn't come back again that night.

Ten

It was late. The fire had died down to mere embers. Robbie lay sleeping in his down sleeping bag and Sabrina was beside him. Denver lay back in his own sleeping bag, staring at the pines moving in the wind above them, listening to the song of the mountains at night. He couldn't sleep. All he could do was think about the woman who lay so near and yet so out of reach. The need for her was like an animal eating out his guts from the inside, and yet he wouldn't have her—shouldn't have her—couldn't have her.

"Get over it," he whispered to himself fiercely, but at the same time, he heard Charlie stir. He raised his head and looked toward where she was supposed to be sleeping. His eyes met her bright ones and his resolve melted into a slow grin at her.

"Can't sleep?" he whispered.

She shook her head.

Reaching out, he took her hand in his and gave it a soft tug.

"There's supposed to be a meteor shower tonight," he whispered to her. "Let's go look for shooting stars."

She smiled and nodded, getting up to join him. She still had on her jeans and a sweatshirt, and all she had to do was fasten the buttons on the jeans to be presentable. Before leaving, she glanced back at her sleeping son. He didn't stir, but Sabrina raised her head and gave Charlie a look that said volumes. Sabrina was on guard. While she lived, nothing would hurt the boy. Charlie turned with fresh confidence and joined Denver, climbing the rise beside him until they'd cleared the trees and were in an area where the sky seemed to fill the universe with so many stars, she was almost blinded by the light.

"Is this real?" she asked softly, overcome by the sight of it. "Am I dreaming?"

"It's real," he assured her. "You could almost reach out and snatch a big one from the heavens, couldn't you?"

He showed her how to lie down and concentrate on one section of the sky and watch for the tail streaking across the huge expanse. He lay beside her, their shoulders touching, their heads close.

They were staring at the skies, but her attention couldn't focus at first. The sense of him beside her was all she could feel. His hand strayed over and grasped hers.

"There," he said. "Did you see that one?"

"Where?" She tried to look, but the warmth of his hand was distracting her. His fingers felt strong and hard and she closed her eyes for a moment, savoring him. She couldn't see many shooting stars with her eyes closed.

"Keep watching the same space, you'll see one...there!" his hand tightened on hers. "Did you catch that one?"

She laughed low in her throat. "No," she admitted, turning her face to look at him, feeling a delicious shiver deep inside.

But he was still staring at the skies. "Look right up there by the Big Dipper...."

"Okay," she said, but her gaze lingered on his profile. Why hadn't she noticed it before? The hard, strong jaw, the beautiful nose, the thick hair...

"Hey, you've got to look or you won't catch one."

Catch a falling star. That was what she wanted. Only the star was beside her, not up in the sky. "Okay," she said reluctantly, and turned to look up. Concentrating hard, she stared and stared and didn't see a thing, while he was pointing them out, one after another.

"Denver! That's not fair. You get them all. Let's trade spaces," she said.

He sighed. "Okay. You take my space." He pointed it out to her in the sky. "I'll take everything left of the Little Dipper."

They switched, but it didn't seem to make any difference at first.

"Nothing's happening," Charlie complained, though she'd found a way to move closer to Denver, so that their bodies were touching all up and down their lengths.

"There goes one!"

"Oh," she cried in frustration. "Where?"

"Didn't you see it? It streaked right across your side and—"

"I see one!" Finally she caught on. "Ohmigosh, how beautiful! I can't believe it. There's another!"

Once she'd seen one, the sky seemed to fill with them, and the sight of them filled her with joy. She forgot everything else, reaching up as though she could snatch one as it flared. "Oh, Denver, look!"

He was looking, but the stars had lost their appeal now that he'd turned and taken in her excitement, and it was Charlie he was looking at. She turned and met his gaze and she knew right away that they were starting down a wild river that would be gathering speed as it headed for the whitewater rapids.

For just a moment, she was afraid. She had an impulse to get up and run back to the camp, run away from Denver and memories and the risk she would be taking. But then his hand touched her cheek and she nuzzled into his palm, kissing the center and sighing, and it only seemed natural that they should do this. She turned into his arms and drew him closer, wanting to feel his warmth against her skin, feel his hard male body, taste his desire and send it spinning out of control.

His mouth felt deliciously scary as it probed hers, as though he were looking for answers and she was hiding them. She closed her eyes and let him search. *Find my secrets,* she seemed to be telling him, *And you can have them all. Only love me and I'll be an open book.*

He drew away from her mouth and dropped a quick kiss at her temple, as though he'd heard her message loud and clear and wasn't sure he accepted the consequences.

"Charlie," he whispered softly near her ear. "If you want to go back, you'd better do it now. Because..."

"I know," she said, curling her fingers into his thick hair. Her body was quivering, pulsing in a way she'd never felt before and she knew it was for him. "I know."

But she didn't go back. She couldn't have left him if she'd wanted to. She'd hated Jeff's lovemaking, hated waiting for him to finish what seemed to make him satisfied, but only made her feel like taking a hot shower to wash the memory away. And that, she supposed, was partly because she'd never loved Jeff, not even from the first. She'd married him because she'd been told to, and she'd wanted so badly to do what would make everyone happy. But his kisses had made her wince and his touch had given her the willies. Passion was a thing she'd never known. But since she'd met Denver, she'd begun to think it might not be a cruel and phony mirage after all.

When his hand brushed her skin, every nerve seemed to sigh, and every part of her began a slow melt. When he took her in his arms, her body came alive in a way she'd never known, and she seemed to find new senses of taste, touch, sound and sight to take him in with, to hold him to her and keep a piece of him in her heart.

Was this love? Or was she just finally reacting to him the way a woman would to any attractive man? How could she know for sure?

But thoughts and hesitations evaporated as his hands slid beneath her sweatshirt and pushed away the fabric so that her breasts were exposed to the cool evening breeze and she arched into his touch, crying out when his hot mouth covered one nipple. Shock-wave sensations cascaded through her and she wanted things she'd never wanted before, wanted them with an urgency that made her blush, wanted them with an animal hunger that almost made her growl.

She couldn't remember how they both wriggled out of their clothes, but suddenly there they were, naked in the moonlight, and she was accepting him, urging him on, reaching for the elusive ecstasy with every thrust he made inside her, knowing there was something waiting for her, something she'd never found before, until finally, there it was and she cried out in joy and fulfillment, cried out and clung to him, churned against him, as though somehow she could make their bodies fuse into one.

She held the feeling to her as it faded, catching every tiny bit of it as a child might catch raindrops on her tongue, savoring even the smallest, most fleeting drop. And then she lay very still, her eyes closed, and she drifted on a milky way of tenderness. She'd never felt this way before, and if she never did again, at least she'd found out what love was all about.

"A shooting star," she murmured, laughing softly.

"What?" He propped himself up on one elbow and looked down at her, his eyes glittering as though they were filled with stars themselves.

"Nothing," she told him, reaching up to trace a path from his temple to his hard chin line. Why bother to talk? Words couldn't describe what she felt. She wanted to bask in it, fill her head and her soul with it, until she could be sure it was real.

His hand trailed a lovely necklace of shivers down across her bare stomach, down to where she was still throbbing, and she gasped, drawing in her breath so sharply, her eyes widened with it. She could take him again, she realized, take him right now and feel that feeling again.

His laugh was soft with affection. "Who would have believed you'd turn into a wanton hussy at the drop of a hat?" he murmured, leaning down to drop tiny kisses around her ear. "I think we could spend the night here and do it again and again and…"

She grabbed his hand to stop those feelings from building. "No," she said breathlessly, regretful but determined. "I've got to get back to Robbie."

"I know," he said, drawing back to look into her face. He stared down at her for a long moment, then asked, "Tell me something, Charlie. What really happened to Robbie's dad?"

A shudder went down her back and she reached for her clothes. Why was he asking that? Why now? She resisted, frowning as she pulled on her sweatshirt, but then she stopped herself. Of course he wanted to know. He had a right to, after what they'd shared. He was going to have to hear about it sometime. Why not now?

"What happened is just what I tell Robbie," she said crisply as she slipped into her jeans. "I wouldn't lie to my boy. Jeff died before he was born." She glanced at him. "Though he was still very much alive when I ran away from him."

There was silence for a moment. Was he just digesting the information, or was he trying to get up enough nerve to ask her a harder question? She wasn't sure. It wouldn't be easy to explain to a man like Denver how she'd acquiesced to her parents' will, how she'd married a man she didn't love, a man who didn't love her, because his family needed the money her family provided, and her family liked the old money name his now-impoverished family provided.

"Why did you run away?" Denver was asking. "Did he..."

"He didn't hit me or anything like that. I ran away because I couldn't bear to stay any longer."

He was silent again and she hoped he was finished with this line. She didn't like to remember those sad and lonely days. Her only freedom had come when she'd left.

"So he died. How did it happen?" he asked her at last.

That one was easy. "A motorcycle accident. Jeff liked fast vehicles and faster women." She smiled, remembering how much that had hurt her at first, hoping her tone didn't sound bitter. She'd found out about his death from an article in a newspaper someone had brought into the Pali and left on the counter. She'd skimmed through the paper and there it had been. Motorcyclist Killed in Freak Accident. She shook her head. "I always told him he would drive himself over a cliff, one way or another, and by golly, one day he did."

Denver turned so that he could see her face. He wanted to know if her words were real or a cover for her feelings. Her eyes told him all he needed to know. She was harboring no secret longing for Robbie's father. If she had at one time, that feeling had died long ago.

But that brought up another question. "Then, if he's not a problem any longer, why can't you go back and face your mother?"

"My mother." She lifted her chin and tried to

smile. "My mother *was* me for large portions of my life. Or at least, she tried to be."

He remembered the woman, though vaguely. She'd been tall, imposing, a Queen Victoria type he could imagine presiding over fox hunts and garden parties, glaring at the serving girl who dropped the crumpets in the grass, telling the butler, "That will be all, Jeeves." A formidable figure—but Charlie had grown up with her. Surely she had some clue as to how to deal with her. "Why would you need to run away from your own mother?"

Charlie was silent. How did you explain something like this to someone who had never experienced it? How could she tell him about the hold her mother had once had on her? How could she describe the way her mother could manipulate her at will? The way the woman had made her childhood miserable?

From the outside, her family had looked so perfect. Her father was a hardworking banker who'd amassed a fortune to add onto the fortune he'd inherited. Her mother had come from simpler roots, but she'd been bound and determined to make everyone forget it. They'd both given Charlie everything she wanted or needed. She knew there were people who'd envied her. But would they have felt the same way if they'd seen her cry herself to sleep at night, knowing she'd spent another day doing everything wrong, disappointing her father and embarrassing her mother?

"I used to think I'd been born into the wrong family," she told him at last. "I struggled every day to be what they wanted. But what they wanted wasn't what I was."

"Okay," he said quietly. "That's fair enough. But if they weren't cruel to you, didn't hurt you…"

She laughed softly. "I told you words can hurt. I know that by experience."

He moved restlessly. "Maybe you should go back and see if things are still the same. After all, you've been gone for a long time. A lot can change."

The thought of going back made her wince. "I can't go back," she insisted. "That part of my life is over."

He didn't answer and she took a deep breath, steadying herself. Reaching over, she kissed him on the cheek. "And that's all the soul-searching I want to do tonight." She pushed up on her knees. "I want to get back to Robbie. Sabrina's a great baby-sitter, but she is only a dog, after all, and you never know when Peter Pan might come flying in to tempt him away. I can't leave him in her care forever."

He watched her leave before he rolled to a sitting position, and then rose to his feet. He'd done what he'd promised himself he would never do, and now he was going to have to pay for it. He'd learned early in life that if you held on too tightly, you might lose the thing you love the most. If you wanted something too badly, you didn't get it. He shouldn't have done this, shouldn't be feeling this way. His most keenly honed instinct was for self-preservation, and that instinct was glowing bright red right now.

Funny, but that thought didn't seem to bring on the usual sense of regret. Maybe he was getting old.

Or maybe this was different.

No. Nothing was ever different. He was a fool if he counted on that. He had to stop this thing before it burrowed so deep inside him he could never be free of it again. He was going to get them where they were going, and then he was going to walk out of her life

and never look back. It had to be that way. There was
no choice.

She'd worried as she tried to fall asleep in her own
sleeping bag. She'd wondered how she was going to
face him in the morning. Should she act natural? Yes,
of course. And she should try not to presume this had
begun a new phase of their relationship. After all, you
never did know....

She dreamed that she was reaching up into a starry
sky, trying to catch a shooting star that stayed frus-
tratingly out of her grasp, and as it flew past, she could
see that Denver was riding on it, laughing down at her
futile attempts to catch him. It was still clear in her
mind when she awoke and she frowned, wondering
why. After all, she had no intention of trying to cap-
ture Denver, and she knew chances were slim even if
she'd wanted to. He was a lone wolf, a man who cherished his freedom more than he cherished anything
else in life. No woman was going to tie him down.
Besides—

No. She'd been about to remind herself that he
didn't like children very much, but that wasn't true
any longer. There was a bond growing between him
and her son that was going to worry her if it got much
stronger. The worst thing she could do to a boy like
Robbie was to have men come in and out of his life,
disappointing him time and again, making him lose
the courage to hope. She'd always been careful not to
let that happen. She couldn't let it happen now, just
because she was in love with the man.

"Love," she whispered, hugging it close and rev-
eling in it. It was so good. She wished she could hold
on to it forever.

But that emotion faded soon enough. Denver was up with the sun and seemed grumpy. He didn't meet her gaze once during breakfast. Was he regretting what they'd done? How dare he! A flash of anger shot through her every time she thought of it. Didn't he see that she'd given him everything she possibly could? Didn't he appreciate it, at least?

They came face-to-face as they cleaned up camp. Denver looked into her violet eyes and winced.

"What happened last night shouldn't have happened," he said shortly, looking away.

She blinked, not expecting that but willing to concede the point. "You're right."

He glanced at her and then looked away quickly, as though he didn't dare look too long. "It's not going to happen again," he declared, turning on his heel.

"You're wrong," she whispered, but he was already out of earshot, and the anger flared in her again.

She calmed down once they got under way. After all, what did last night mean to him? He'd no doubt had a hundred girls, each one more casually than the last. He couldn't help it that he was the only man she'd ever made love to—ever *really* made love to. She was just one more woman to him. How could he know that he was so special to her? Why should he care?

She'd worked herself into a state of misery by the time they made their first rest stop. Robbie and Sabrina ran down to the river, but she and Denver stayed in the shade of a stand of aspen. They sat side by side, neither saying a word. Finally she turned to him, putting her hand on his arm just above the elbow.

"Denver," she began.

But she never finished her sentence. At her touch, he jerked away and she could feel something—

whether a quiver or a shiver or a trembling, she couldn't be sure. But he'd definitely reacted to her, and her surprise struck her voiceless.

She thought he was going to jump up and walk away, but that didn't happen. Instead, he turned back and looked into her eyes for a moment. Then he reached out and drew her close, and before she understood what was going on he was kissing her, kissing her deeply, wildly, as though he had to prove something to her—or maybe to himself.

The kiss was short. He broke away from her quickly enough. But that kiss said volumes to her and when he rose and left her, following Robbie to the river, she stayed behind, feeling breathless, her heart beating like something untamed in her chest. Her mouth felt bruised and she put a hand to her lips, wanting to feel what it had been like again. Closing her eyes, she relived it. Lord, but she loved this man! How was she going to prove it to him?

They didn't rest much longer, and once they started up again, they lasted for two and a half hours. Denver didn't speak to her or look at her as they traveled, but this time it didn't matter that much. She could feel him, sense him, know when he was near, when he was thinking about her, too. And he was thinking about her a lot. He wanted to kiss her again, to touch her, to make love the way they'd made love the night before. It was in the air between them, and it made her blood sing in her veins and made her heart as light as a feather. The color of the sky was bluer, the birds sounded sweeter, the water ran clearer. Life was just more intense when you were in love.

"In love." Those words would have frightened her just a few days before. Now, they represented her life.

They stopped in an open meadow, leaning against the huge, rough trunk of a fallen pine. Robbie only needed about thirty seconds' rest and he was up and running again, looking for frogs in the soggy grass, but even Sabrina was too tired to join him. She lay down, put her head on her forepaws and closed her eyes. Charlie and Denver leaned side by side without saying a word, listening to the hum of bees and the rustle of leaves in the breeze.

Charlie felt limp as a rag doll. The day was warmer and the hike was beginning to get to her. But more than that, the man beside her was constantly on her mind. He wasn't going to be around much longer. She really ought to find out all she could while she had the chance. She knew he didn't want to talk to her, but she was determined, and she turned to gaze at him with chin held high.

"Denver, tell me this," she said to him. "What do you have against women?"

"Women?" He looked at her, surprised. "I don't have anything against women. I like women."

She shook her head firmly. "No, you don't."

A patient look came over his handsome face and he turned, leaning one shoulder against the log. "Okay, I can see you're dying to tell me all about myself. Why don't I like women?"

She frowned, studying him. "That's what I'm trying to figure out. There's a lot of evidence, but no real conclusion." She narrowed her eyes. "There's no woman in your life right now, and you haven't mentioned any woman who's important to you. You hold me at arm's length. You seem to push women away. Even Gail..."

His face changed and his jaw hardened. "Gail. What does this have to do with my sister?"

She searched his eyes. "I remember how Gail used to be about you," she said softly. "She adored you."

He rubbed his chin with the palm of his hand and looked away. "I don't want to talk about Gail."

She ignored his words. "She talked about you all the time," she went on, as though she hadn't heard him. "You were like—father, brother, benefactor, best friend, all rolled into one. She was always trying to find ways to thank you." She paused, wondering if she was going too far. But his face told her he wasn't going to protest again, that he was listening, and she went on. "Remember the cookies she used to send you? And the brownies?"

He couldn't help it. His smile was edging through. "You mean those brown rubber things she sent me?" he asked.

She laughed, so glad he was warming up. "That's them. We all sneaked down into the kitchen after curfew and baked them together, whispering and giggling in the semidarkness."

He almost grinned. "I kept them around for paper weights. They still looked the same three years later."

Charlie laughed again, then sobered quickly. "She loved you so much. Denver, tell me what happened."

He didn't say anything for so long, she thought he was going to ignore the question. But finally, he spoke softly. "Gail was my life. After our parents died, we only had each other, and we had our dreams. We both worked so hard to make them come true. I made the money so that she could go to any school she wanted, and she worked hard, making the grades. We were a team. We knew where we were going."

"I know," she told him, her heart full. "Gail told us all about it. She was going to go to medical school..."

His face brightened. "See? You knew about it, didn't you? She *did* want it then. I know she did."

Charlie nodded. "I think so. I know she thought so when we were in school together."

"She did. Even through her junior year in college, she still wanted it. And then she met—"

He stopped himself and she had the distinct impression he'd been about to call someone a very nasty name.

"She met Ricky," he amended. "Ricky, with the long hair and the tattoo on his neck and the motorcycle and the guitar."

So that was it. Charlie took a deep breath and let it out again. The eternal story. It happened every time. "She fell in love?"

He gave her a scornful look. "He hypnotized her. How could she love scum like that? A girl like Gail..." His voice wavered and he stopped for a moment, then came back stronger than ever. "She ran off with him. Ruined her life. Ruined everything we'd planned. Threw it all away for a ride on a motorcycle." He shrugged, pushing the emotion away. "So that's over. Gail is out of my life."

Charlie's heart broke for them both, but this story shed a bit of light on his distrust. He'd dedicated his life to raising his sister up to some shining standard, and when she'd turned her back on his dream, he'd felt betrayed. Maybe that was what made him so suspicious of closeness now. Maybe he thought his love would always be thrown back in his face. "Has she tried to contact you since—?"

His face was hard again. "Charlie, I don't want to talk about it, okay? You know what happened. Now we can forget it."

She bit her tongue and followed him as he straightened and started back toward the trail again. Gail had been a good friend. No matter what she'd done, Charlie knew Gail still loved her brother. And Denver made it obvious that he still cared about her, cared so much, it tore him apart to be like this. Right then and there she made a promise to herself. She was going to get the two of them back together again. Somehow. Someday.

"You always hurt the one you love." The old saying kept floating through her mind. It had always mystified her, but now she had a sudden perception of what it meant. "The one you love is the only one you *can* hurt," she whispered to herself. "The one you love is the one who counts."

They hiked on for another hour and then came to a stream where they stopped to wash their faces and drink from their canteens. Denver looked around the area and pulled out the map, studying it for a moment before folding it and putting it away again.

"You two stay here and rest. Maybe put together some food for us in about half an hour. I'm going to scout on ahead. If we've followed the map correctly, it should be just over that next rise. I'll check it out."

"What should be over there?" she asked, too tired to really care.

"The place we're going to," he answered, forcing back a smile as his gaze flickered over her. There was no reason not to tell her where they were going, but he couldn't resist teasing her a little.

Looking at him, she could see his game and she

sighed, looking away. She didn't really care where it was they were going. She only cared that they were almost there. She knew that when they got there, her time with him would be almost over. He wouldn't be staying after he led them home again. Why on earth would he? He had his own life to live.

She watched him go until he was out of sight. Sabrina got up, rested, and dashed off with him, but Robbie came in to join her. They sat and listened to the sound of the river and soon they were dozing. She wasn't sure how much time had elapsed when she woke with a start. Something had woken her. She wasn't sure what it was. Rising, she went to the backpacks and rummaged for a tissue. There was a sound and she straightened. And that was when she saw it.

A huge brown bear was lumbering toward their resting place, sauntering along as though it owned the mountain and considered interlopers merely annoying. A scream rose in her throat, but it didn't come out. She looked quickly at where Robbie still slept, and she didn't know if it would be better to wake him and tell him to run, or to leave him sleep and hope the bear didn't notice him. And then it was too late for decisions, because the bear had noticed her. It stopped, raised its head and seemed to sniff the air. But its gaze was riveted to Charlie.

Her heart thumped in her chest as though it wanted to burst out. She couldn't run. She knew she couldn't climb a tree fast enough to make a difference. For the first time in her life, she wished for a gun. But she didn't have one. The only thing she could think to do was reach into the backpack and hope to find something. She reached, and her fingers encountered something hard and round. There was one can of beef stew left, and luckily, she'd found it. Grabbing hold, she pulled it out and hefted it in her hand. The bear was coming closer, glaring at her with its sharp, disinterested brown eyes. One slap of that huge paw, and she would be flat on her back.

I'm like a piece of meat to him, she thought, looking into those cold eyes. *I'm nothing. I'm expendable.*

The animal would make short work of her. And then it might notice Robbie.

Not Robbie. Anger rose to overwhelm the fear, and she raised the can threateningly. "Get out of here," she yelled at the bear. "Get out, or I'll throw this at you!"

Only a few yards away, the bear cocked its head, then began to rise on its hind feet. The effect was terrifying. It looked as big as a house.

"Go!" she yelled again, and then, with all her might, she threw the can of stew at the bear's head.

The can landed right on the bear's nose and bounced away again. The animal reared back, and made a whimpering noise, like a surprised dog. Charlie held her breath. If he came at her now, she didn't have a clue what she would do. The animal seemed to take forever to make up its mind, but finally it did. Growling, it turned, lumbering off through the underbrush, making complaining noises as it went.

Charlie stared after it, her breath coming in short, painful gasps. She'd won. She'd faced down a bear and won. She could hardly believe it.

And neither could Denver, when he returned and she related the story, not leaving out a detail or an emotion.

"You held off a bear with a can of stew?" he kept repeating, looking at her as though she were someone he hadn't met before. "My God. You must have thrown with authority."

All in all, she was pretty proud of herself. Robbie was outraged that he hadn't been awake to see it, but he thought his mother was pretty cool. They ate lunch and talked and laughed about it, then prepared to continue their trip. Denver had seen the end of their journey ahead. He thought they could make it in a couple of hours.

"Couldn't we just sort of circle around the place for a few days?" she asked Denver wistfully as she gathered her things.

He stared down at her, amusement fading. "And continue this hell that much longer?" he asked her softly.

She looked up at him. "You found this trip hell?" she asked in surprise.

"In spades," he muttered, shaking his head, his eyes dark. "I want it over with."

She moved closer, wanting to understand. "What's been so awful?" she asked him.

He hesitated. Reaching out, he touched her golden hair. "It's hell being with you like this," he told her, speaking softly so that Robbie wouldn't hear them as he played with Sabrina at the water's edge. "You're there all the time, but I can't touch you." He hesitated, then muttered a soft obscenity and began to turn away. "I swore I wouldn't get into this with you."

She stopped him with a hand on his arm. "Into what?" she asked, feeling breathless.

He stared at her, his eyes as deep as mountain lakes. "Wanting you this way," he whispered.

She stared back. Was that all there was to it? Was it really her he wanted? Or just… "If that's all you need," she said evenly, her eyes challenging him, "I'm sure there are some girls somewhere who can take care of you."

His large hand was suddenly grasping her shoulder, pulling her closer. "I don't want 'some girls,'" he told her softly. "You know what I want. I want you."

She knew he did, but still, she resented his attitude. After all, did he think he was the only one who was yearning for something he couldn't have? "You don't have to act like it's a curse."

He dropped his hand, shaking his head, half laughing. "I was a perfectly happy man before I met you."

She glared at him. "And now you're miserable. Is that it?"

"Damn right," he said loudly, his voice carrying as Robbie came running back to join them.

She glared at him even harder. "No swearing," she said out of the side of her mouth.

"Don't worry," he told her as he turned away. "Me and my swearing will be out of your hair soon enough." And he headed out toward the rise.

She watched him go and wondered. What would it have been like if she'd married him instead of Jeff?

I never would have done that, she told herself. My mother would never have allowed it. After all, she had Jeff picked out for me by the time I was ten years old.

People and their dreams. Maybe they ought to learn to keep them to themselves.

Eleven

They arrived at their destination two hours later and in the end, it did surprise Charlie. She'd expected an abandoned miner's hut or a hunters' supply shack, but what they found was a beautiful log cabin that was very much in use, surrounded by well-tended gardens, a chicken coop and a goat pen. Smoke was rising from the chimney. All in all, it couldn't have been more inviting.

"This is supposed to be owned by a woman named Goldie," Denver told her as they walked up to the doorway.

"Goldie? You're kidding!"

"Do you know her?"

"Of course. She's an old friend." Charlie hesitated on the doorstep. "But what is she going to think of us barging in on her this way?"

The door opened and Goldie's beaming face was

her answer. "You took your time," she told her guests tartly. "I was expecting you by lunch. I make that hike a lot faster than you did."

Charlie gave her a hug, laughing. "But how did you know we were coming?"

Goldie shrugged. "Ernie gave me a call on my cell phone. I can get cell service for about two hours, just before noon every day."

"Ernie knew?" Charlie turned and looked questioningly at Denver. "How did Ernie know?"

"I talked to him before we left," he told her. "Practically everyone in town was in on it by the time we got going." He shook his head, almost smiling again. "You don't really think they didn't recognize that picture that was being handed around, do you?"

"What?" She was bewildered. "What do you mean?"

"Everyone knew it was you. They all wanted to protect you." He laughed shortly. "Hey, everyone loves you in that town."

She stared at him. "Do they?" she said weakly, completely and utterly surprised.

"Sure. They had no idea who it was that wanted you, but they figured it was up to you to deal with it, and they were ready to do what they could to help you avoid the investigator." He grinned at her perplexed look. "Where do you think I got the map to get to this place? It wasn't my idea. Ernie had talked it over with a bunch of other people and they'd all decided this was the best place for you to hide out for a while."

"Wow." She sank into a chair and fought the tears that threatened. So often she'd felt completely alone.

Now it looked as if that had been a dumb thing to feel. "What a great bunch of people."

Denver watched her, read the emotions shifting in her face, and something touched him inside as well. Connections. He'd always scorned them in the past. But he was gaining a new respect. Family. Community. They were more than just hollow words. Done right, they meant something.

"You've done a lot for others in your time, Charlie," Goldie was saying, bustling about to make them comfortable. "And everyone admires the way you've been raising that boy all by yourself. We all wanted to let you know how much we care for you."

Charlie was stunned. She'd had no idea, and somehow just knowing how good people could be made her humble.

"It's so nice of you to let us stay," she began, but Goldie waved her words away.

"Are you kidding? I'm glad for the company. I like it up here alone, but having good folks around for a spell never hurts. You all can stay for as long as you need to."

Goldie fed them a magnificent meal of fried chicken and squash from her garden and regaled them with anecdotes about her beloved research subjects. And that turned out to be pocket gophers. She had pictures and carvings and sketches of the little beasts all over her home.

"They're cute, huh?" Robbie noted.

Goldie's lower lip protruded. "Cute? Not a bit of it. They are anything but; when you get to know them." She looked at the boy. "Tomorrow I'll take you out to my research area and show you what they're like. I've got an underground observation post set up with a huge glass panel, so we can see right into their burrows.''

"Like an ant farm?" Robbie asked, and she nodded.

"Goldie, what got you interested in these gopher creatures?" Charlie asked her at last, remembering about her trip to see her son. "What keeps you up here all year around? It must get so lonely.''

"Not for me," she responded briskly. "I hang around with pocket gophers mainly because they're not people.''

"You're anti-people?"

"Yup. Long experience has taught me to stay away from people. They always disappoint you. They always disappear when you need them most. They never do what they say they're going to.'' She shook her head at the sorry state of the human race. "But gophers—you can count on those little rascals to do just about what you would predict they'll do. They always come through for you. They act just like you expect them to.''

For some reason that made Charlie think of her mother. She knew she'd always disappointed her, that she'd never done what her mother had expected of her. Funny. She'd never really thought of it from her mother's point of view before. Things did look different from the other side.

She had to be careful not to do that to Robbie—not to try to mold him and hound him into being what she wanted. That didn't mean she wouldn't maintain standards and have certain expectations of behavior. But his personality was his own and she was constantly reminding herself to leave it to him. He was who he was.

After eating, they sat around and talked a little

longer. Robbie looked sleepy. Denver went back to looking remote. And Charlie could hardly keep her eyes open.

"It's bedtime, I see," Goldie announced, rising energetically. "You're in luck. I've got a spare bedroom." She led the way and Charlie and Denver followed along behind, avoiding each other's eyes.

"Now you two can sleep in here—" Goldie began, pointing out the big, comforter-covered bed that almost filled the little room.

"Oh no!" Charlie said, stepping back inadvertently, glancing at Denver and then away again quickly.

"What's wrong?" Goldie asked. "You see a rattler in the bedclothes or something?"

"No—uh—" She glanced at Denver again. "Listen, Goldie. We don't sleep together. We can't share a bed."

Goldie frowned over the arch in her nose at them, peering through her rimless glasses. "That so? I thought the two of you were married."

"No," Charlie said quickly.

"Yes, but—" Denver began at the same time.

They looked at each other and both shook their heads.

"No," Denver amended.

"Yes, but—" Charlie began, then stopped and started again. "I'm sorry, Goldie," she said. "It's just too complicated to explain. But we aren't sleeping together."

Goldie nodded, looking bewildered but too wise to try to figure it out. "Oh, sure, I get it. You're a couple, but you ain't married. Or, you're married, but you ain't a couple. I get it." She shook her head. "Believe me, this is not uncommon. Now, in the pocket gopher world..."

"About the sleeping arrangements?" Denver broke in hurriedly. He could feel another long lecture about gopher habits coming on.

"Okay," she said accommodatingly. "Then how about Charlie and the boy on the bed, Denver on the couch. Will that work for you?"

"Yes," they both said in unison and with relief. "That will be fine."

And it was. They were all three so tired they slept like logs and didn't wake up until Goldie had been rattling pans in the kitchen for some time the next morning. They rose slowly, lazily, glad to be inside for a change, and then sat down to eat the home-baked bread and fresh eggs Goldie had scrambled up for them. Conversation was slow and superficial. But by the time they'd finished eating, Charlie knew she had to bring up the question that was most on her mind.

"How long will you be staying?" she asked Denver.

"I think I'd better rest my knee for a day," he answered, avoiding her gaze. "I'll probably get out of your hair by tomorrow morning."

Tomorrow morning. She looked down at her plate so that he wouldn't see the regret in her eyes. One more day and then he would be gone. She might never see him again.

Inexplicably, instead of drawing them closer, that thought seemed to send them back into the adversarial position they'd flirted with before. As the morning drifted away, they found more and more things to argue about. After Denver had chastised her for losing his map, which he immediately found exactly where he'd put it to keep it safe, she sighed and shook her head.

"I'm thinking about finding some liquor and getting you drunk," she told him evenly.

He turned and looked at her, surprised and somewhat annoyed. "Why?"

She paused, then smiled at him, enjoying the way his thick hair was falling over his blue eyes. "You were cute drunk," she told him softly.

He didn't weaken. "Getting drunk is stupid."

"I know. But you're so much friendlier when you're sloshed."

She stared into his eyes and something stirred in their depths. But he managed to cover it up right away, and another chance was lost. As she watched him walk away from her, into the kitchen, she began to feel desperate. There wasn't much time left. Why were they wasting it this way?

Goldie seemed to be thinking the same thing. She came in from showing Robbie the goats with a plan in mind. "I'm taking Robbie out to my meadow to see my pocket gophers," she announced, reaching for her walking shoes. "He needs an excursion."

"I'll go with you," Denver said, reaching for his jacket.

But Goldie put up a hand to stop him, looking stern. "No, you won't. You stay right here."

He turned, frowning as Charlie came up behind him, curious about what was going on. "Why? What's the matter?"

Goldie clucked at him, shaking her head. "I've got eyes, haven't I? I can feel the tension between the two of you. You both need to talk this out without your boy around to hear you."

"We've talked too much as it is," he grumbled, protesting.

Goldie snorted and waved a hand in the air as she turned to go. "Time you both talked the same language. I can tell. I've seen enough interpersonal relationships between my gophers to read the signs." She turned back and looked at them from the doorway. "You two are going to have exactly two hours to get this settled between you. And when I get back, I don't want to see any more sparks flying. You got that?"

Denver gave her a crooked grin. "Aye-aye, Captain," he said.

The door closed and they looked at each other warily. Charlie's heart began a steady drumbeat in her chest.

"Friend or foe?" she asked him, only half joking.

He stared at her, shaking his head. "The best thing we could do," he stated coolly, "would be to stay out of each other's way until I manage to get out of here."

"Are you serious?" she asked, amazed at him.

"Yes, I'm very serious. I just want to get away without making any more of a mess than I already have."

A mess! What was he thinking? She searched his gaze, trying to figure him out, but he turned away.

"Look, I'm really tired," he said, stretching his back. "I want to get some more sleep. Mind if I use your bed? Then I'll be out of your way and you can do whatever you want out here."

"Want some company?" she asked softly, making one last valiant try.

"Charlie, don't," he said, grimacing.

Anger shot through her like a Fourth-of-July fireworks display, but she managed to keep the evidence out of her voice. "What's the problem? I'm standing right here and we're all alone. You can touch me now."

He looked at her, then quickly away again. "No. I tried that before."

She frowned. "What do you mean by that?"

He hesitated, then shrugged and told her. "I thought maybe if we made love I could get you out of my mind. But it only made things worse."

Her eyes flashed. She'd had just about enough of this. "You almost act as though this is all to do with some biological urge and there's nothing else to it," she accused him.

He nodded slowly, looking dark, troubled. "I don't want to think there's anything else to it."

"Can't face the truth, can you?" she said softly, but it was all bravado. She didn't know what the truth was. Maybe he did only like her for the lovemaking. Maybe that was all there ever was for him.

It was different for her. The lovemaking was only the icing on the cake, a way of showing him how she felt inside. There could be no lovemaking without the love. But maybe men didn't see it that way.

"Never mind," she said crisply, reaching for a towel. "You go on and take your nap. I'm going to take a shower."

The shower was outside in its own little shed. Goldie collected rain water in a reservoir and had a generator-driven water heater. Charlie turned the water on and closed her eyes. She could either cry, or tough it out and make a plan. Now all she had to do was decide which was more likely to get her what she wanted.

Denver was trying to sleep, but it was no use. He knew that one insignificant log cabin wall away, Charlie was naked. The thought of it was enough to make him writhe. Then the water started, and he couldn't get the picture of those cool, silvery drops sliding over her body out of his mind. To make things worse, she began to sing. He looked around for something to cover his ears with, but he couldn't get away from it. She was everywhere, in his thoughts, in his senses. It was as though she now inhabited his bloodstream.

He was going to have to get out of here. He couldn't wait until tomorrow. He had to go now. Rising from the bed, he looked around the room, trying to calculate what he needed to pack to get going. There wasn't much, but he would need some food. He supposed he would have to wait until Robbie came back. He couldn't go off without saying goodbye to the boy. If he could just hold out until then…

He glanced out the window. Charlie had finished her shower and she was out in the yard, picking wild flowers and putting them in her damp hair. If that weren't bad enough, her attire really got to him. She was wrapped in the abbreviated towel and that was all. She looked like some fairy princess, frolicking in her kingdom.

She couldn't prance around like that. What was she thinking? He opened the door and called to her.

"Charlie! Come on in the house. You can't go outside dressed like that."

She raised her head and smiled at him, waving. "Why not?" she asked simply. "There's no one here but us. Not for miles and miles." She laughed at him as she spun around, arms outstretched, towel sagging. "In fact, if I wanted to go naked…" Her hand went to the tuck just above her breast.

"No!" he cried, leaving the doorway and striding toward her. If she wasn't going to behave, he was going to have to take matters into his own hands.

"What's the matter, Denver?" she said, gently taunting him. "Afraid of a little flesh?"

He knew she wasn't going to come quietly and he didn't waste time with that. Instead, he swept her up into his arms the moment he reached her, trying to hold her with authority rather than romance in mind.

"Oh!" she cried as he swung her up. "Denver!"

He turned back toward the house, his face set with determination. He was going to be as impersonal as he could.

"Whoops," she said softly as her towel fell open. "Oh Denver, look what you've done."

Looking at her was the last thing he meant to do, but she was laughing and clinging to his neck and she was so beautiful, her round breasts creamy white in the sunlight, her body long and lean and made for love. He knew it was all over by the time he got her into the house, and he barely got the door kicked closed before he was devouring her. They writhed together this time, her naked body against him as he fell with her on the bed. There was no time to think. He had to have her as he had to have air to breathe and he took her as though he'd conquered her, though he knew the truth was just the opposite.

She cried out and held him to her, wrapping her long legs around his hips, driving him deeper and deeper inside her, as though she wanted to take in every bit of him and never let him go again, until they were both spent, lying back and fighting for breath.

"Now tell me that was only physical," she demanded in a low, husky voice. "You just try to tell me you don't feel anything for me at all. That all you want is—"

His mouth covered hers, smothering out her words. He couldn't tell her any such thing, but neither could he tell her that he had never felt for another woman what he felt for her. Because, though it was true, it didn't matter. They had no future. He couldn't pretend they did.

They made love again, because after all, they only had the two hours and the minutes were speeding away.

"Are you still leaving tomorrow?" she asked him softly, her head cradled in the protection of his shoulder.

"Yes," he said, his arm tightening around her. "What are you planning to do?"

What was she planning to do? It was funny, but she hadn't really thought about it. Her mind and heart had been consumed with thoughts of Denver. There hadn't been room for anything else.

"I guess I'll stay here until…"

"Until what?"

She shrugged. "I don't know. Until Ernie says it's safe to go home, I guess."

He turned and looked at her. "It won't ever be safe. Come on, Charlie. You're a bright lady. You know that."

She did know it, but she didn't know what she could do about it. She'd been living with the knowledge that this couldn't last forever, and in the last few days, that had turned from conjecture to reality. She was going to have to face that fact.

They dressed and went into the kitchen. She put some water on for tea and leaned against the counter, her arms crossed over her chest as though she were cold, even though it was a mild day. He sat at the kitchen table and ate an apple.

"What do you think I should do?" she asked him, hoping he'd have a great new idea but knowing there just might not be one.

He looked at her for a long time, crunching on the apple, before answering. Then he spoke slowly. "I think you should go back to San Francisco and face your mother," he told her frankly.

"What?" She drew her arms in more closely. That was not a solution to anything. He just didn't understand.

Denver rose, tossed away the apple core, and took hold of her shoulders to make her stay and listen to him. "Charlie, you can handle your mother now. You're a different person from the frightened girl who ran away and ended up in a mountain valley. You have a child. You've made your own way in the world, without any help from your family. You're ready to go back. You're stronger than you think."

She turned her face away. This was not the advice she'd wanted to hear.

Reaching around her, Denver took something from the cupboard behind her and held it in his hand. "Here you go, Charlie." He handed her a can of beef stew. "If you can handle a brown bear out in the wilderness, you can handle your mother. Believe in yourself, for God's sake."

She looked at the can and began to laugh. "Come to think of it," she admitted, "that bear coming toward me did look a lot like my mother."

He nodded, leaning against the counter beside her. "You faced the bear. Charlie, you can do anything."

She held the can up and looked at it, smiling but shaking her head. "I don't know…"

"Charlie." He took her chin in his hand. "Why don't you and Robbie come on back with me tomorrow? You can visit your mother and see how the land lies."

She sighed, but she didn't say anything.

He put a finger under her chin and tilted her face up for a kiss. "Charlie," he told her softly. "You're not alone."

She blinked in surprise. Did he mean—?

But no, he didn't.

"You have to think about Robbie," he said. "He deserves a mother who can stand up for herself."

She didn't answer, but she mulled over everything he'd said. She knew he was right. How had he become so smart, anyway? So smart, it seemed, about everything but his own sister. Strange how it was always so much easier to give advice than to take it.

By the time she looked out the window and could see Robbie and Goldie returning from the meadow, she'd made up her mind. Though it pained her to admit it, Denver was right. He'd said the things she should have been saying to herself. It was time to stop hiding. She was going back. She was going to face her mother. There was no telling how this was going to come out, but she had to do it.

Turning to Denver, she reached up and put her arms around his neck, then kissed him soundly on the mouth. He got the message.

"Good," he said, but as she turned away to greet the explorers, he stayed behind and watched her go. He knew he wanted her more than he'd ever wanted any other woman—wanted the whole of her. If she stayed here, if she didn't go back, he might even have a chance of having her. Instead, he'd just convinced her to go back to the kind of life she'd come from, the sort of people he could never join, the sort of existence he could never share. Was he crazy?

Maybe not crazy. But definitely a masochist.

Denver was in the hospital and feeling very grumpy. It had been almost two weeks since he'd hiked out of the wilderness with Charlie and Robbie and packed them into a bus to San Francisco. She'd left and he'd stayed. Funny how things worked out.

He'd torn the knee to shreds with all that climbing, just as he'd known he probably would. It had taken a series of operations at the local hospital to get it back in shape. They said, given a little time, it would be almost as good as new.

"Desk job," his boss, Josh, had said when he'd called him. "You're good for at least six months at headquarters, the way things look."

A desk job was not Denver's idea of a decent way to make a living. The thought of it made him very irritable. "I could always quit and go hire on to some foreign country's mercenary force," he'd told Josh. "Most of those places are always on the lookout for a hired gun."

Josh hadn't even tried to argue with him about it. He knew he would never sign on with a country whose agenda he didn't believe in. "You just get better," he'd said. "Then we'll see."

But that had been the plan when he'd first arrived, hadn't it? Sometimes things just didn't turn out the way you thought they would. Something was beginning to tell him he might have to begin looking for another line of work, and doing that cut to the core of what he was, how he saw himself. Thinking about it didn't brighten his spirits at all.

A woman entered the room and he didn't even look up. The parade of nurses in and out had gotten old real fast. Most of them seemed to want to do things he didn't want done, so he tried to ignore this one as long as possible.

She stopped by the side of the bed. "Denver?" she said softly.

He looked up, startled. His gaze met the cool gray eyes of his sister Gail and he blinked, wondering for just a moment if it was a mirage.

"Gail?"

There were tears in her eyes. She nodded and took his hand in hers, and he found himself squeezing very tightly.

He'd thought about this moment. He'd planned all sorts of ways he might speak coldly to her, make her see the error of her ways. But that all fell away. His sister had come to him with love in her eyes and that was all that mattered. His knee was sore, but the rest of him was fine, and he pulled her down into his arms. "Gail. Oh, my God."

There were tears in his eyes, too, and they laughed together, blending hugs and wet kisses and long moments of looking at each other.

"Ricky and I got married," she told him when they got settled enough to speak whole sentences. "I know you thought he was wrong for me, Denver, but he's changed a lot. Wait until you see him. He's cut his hair and he's working as a stockbroker...."

It was too much for him to take in all at once. "How did you know I was here?" he asked her wonderingly.

She smiled at him. "Charlyne. She found me and told me and…"

He didn't hear the rest. Charlie had done this. Of course. Who else?

"She said to tell you it was payback for what you'd done for her."

Sure. Why not?

They talked and made plans to get together again, and then she had to go, because she'd come all this way just for the afternoon. She had to get back.

"To work?" he asked her as she gathered her things and prepared to leave.

"Oh no. To school." She flashed him a big smile. "I finished getting my bachelor's last year. I'm in medical school now." She bent to kiss him goodbye. "See?" she whispered to him. "Never give up on people you love."

He watched her go, her hair bouncing as she walked away, her spirit still filling the room with energy, and he thanked God for Charlie. She'd left a hole in his heart, but she'd given him the rest of his life back.

The rumor was that Charlie wasn't coming back. Everyone was buzzing about it. Some said the cabin had been rented to a retired couple from San Diego, others said that the owner was going to tear it down and build a lodge. All anyone knew for sure was that Charlie's things were being packed to be shipped to her in San Francisco.

It was just as well, Denver supposed. And only natural. She was back among her own kind of people. That was where she belonged.

It took a few days to get used to the idea that he might never see her again, but he managed. It had been almost two months since he'd seen her last. The weather had turned colder. Christmas was only a couple of days away. Snow filled the valley and clung to the mountain, and that was a good thing, because you needed snow if you were going to run a ski lift.

And that was exactly what he was going to do. He'd saved up a lot of money over the years, and now he had something to spend it on. The more he'd thought about going back to work, the more he'd known he had grown beyond the sort of law enforcement work he'd been doing all these years. He needed something new, something different and ambitious. And one day, while walking down to the general store, he'd passed the For Sale sign at the ski lift and the idea had come to him. Why not stay and run the lift? It was just small enough to be manageable, just challenging enough to be interesting.

So here he was on this bright December day, learning the ropes from Hal Waters and loving every minute of it. This was the life. This was just what a man needed to get his mind off…things.

And he'd been doing a pretty good job of it. He'd never needed a woman in his life and he wasn't going to start mooning over one now. There were times, late at night, or sometimes when he heard a hawk cry, that he thought of her and something deep inside him clenched tight and made him want to kick something. But most of the time, he was doing just fine.

And that was exactly what he was telling himself that December day as he walked back from storing the grooming machine, favoring his right knee only slightly now. There was a pretty good crowd queuing up as the lift opened. He looked up at the people, not expecting anything. And there she was, standing in line.

He stopped and stared at her. She was with a crowd of people in expensive ski clothes, carrying the latest European skis, but she caught sight of him just as he saw her, and their gazes locked for a long, electric moment.

"Denver?" she said, asking him something.

"What?" he called back, moving forward and vaulting up onto the ramp. He would have done anything to get to her. Suddenly, that was all life meant to him.

And then he'd reached her. Blond hair cascaded around her shoulders, snowflakes clung to her eyelashes, her cheeks were red, her mouth half open with anticipation and she was smiling up at him, her eyes like a heaven full of stars. The rest of the world might as well have been purple Jell-O for all he noticed it. She was everything.

"Come on," he said, holding a hand out to her.

She took it and they began to walk quickly toward the warming hut. People in her party called to her, but she didn't look back. She held his hand very tightly and followed him, into the hut and then into the suite of rooms at the far end, and finally, into the office he called his own.

He closed the door and turned to her. They crashed together and fused, and he filled his arms with her and she tilted her head back to demand his kiss and they clung together, half laughing, half sobbing, tears mixed with kisses, until they'd spun out of control and were sliding out of their clothes and coming together in a wild few minutes of lovemaking that seemed to rock the world.

She was so slim, so round, so fragile, he tried to go slow, to be careful, but she wouldn't let him. As he slid inside her, she cried out and thrust her hips high, demanding every bit he had to offer. As he took her, churning again and again, white heat became white noise, and there was nothing but the two of them, clinging together as though they could never be pried apart, as though their souls could melt together if they willed it.

"Oh, I missed you," she gasped, trying to catch her breath as they pulled apart at last. "Don't ever leave me like that again."

"I'm not the one who left," he reminded her, nibbling on her neck and sliding his hands down to cup her bottom and settle her back in close against him.

"You're the one who made *me* leave," she told him serenely, luxuriating in his embrace. "I was praying every step of the way that you'd still be here."

His arms tightened around her. He knew for certain now. He loved her. Love for her burned inside him. Without her, he was nothing but a shell of a man. But he wasn't sure about her, how she felt.

"How is it being back among the high-society crowd?" he asked her, pretending to be casual.

She thought for a moment before she answered. "Sort of fun, actually," she told him. "You were right. Things are completely different now. I still find myself jumping to attention every time my mother raises her voice, but I can deal with it. I don't let her push me around. At least, not all the time."

"Good," he said, though he wasn't surprised at all. "I'm glad you got that settled. Now there's one more thing you need to do."

"What is that?"

He took a deep breath. This wasn't easy. He buried his face in her honey-gold hair. "Marry me," he muttered.

"Marry you?" She leaned her head back and gazed at him in wonder. "You're not the marrying kind."

He breathed in her scent. He needed it like he needed oxygen—just to exist. "Marry me anyway. I'll learn."

"But…" She swallowed hard, hating what she had to say to him, and he steeled himself, dread growing, as he read "no" in her face. "Denver, I can't marry you. I told you from the first that Robbie is my first concern. I have to do what I think is best for him. And I…I promised him we would come back here. I'm going to raise him here. Going back to the city only reinforced that. Your job takes you all over the world and I can't drag Robbie—"

"Where is he?"

She hesitated. "We're staying at a condo in town, until we can get the cabin back in shape. He's there right now."

Denver released her and reached for his clothes. "Let's go get him."

She smiled. "He'll be so happy to see you."

He nodded, pulling on his shirt. "Me too." He glanced at his watch. "But I don't have much time. I've got to be back to run the lines by noon."

She frowned, puzzled, then glanced around the office as though she'd finally realized where they were. "What are you doing? Are you working here?"

He pulled her sweater down over her head, kissed her mouth, and grinned at her. "Charlie, I own this place. Or I will once the bank gets through doing its thing. I'm planning to be a permanent resident myself.'' His grin grew cocky. ''So I guess I'll be seeing you around town. But since you won't marry me...''

The squeal she let out was ear-piercing, but the leap into his arms was the part he liked best. He laughed as she clung to him and blubbered unintelligible things against his neck.

''Okay, okay, I'll ask you again,'' he said, surprised at how good it felt to be in love. ''But let's wait until we have Robbie with us.''

She slid down and landed on her feet and he helped her into her jacket, noting the tearstains on her cheeks. Looking up, she gave him a wet smile. ''Do you love me?'' she asked him simply.

He tried to speak but something seemed to be caught in his throat and all he could do was nod.

''Good,'' she said. ''Because I love you so very much.''

She hugged him, then turned impatiently toward the door. ''Let's go,'' she said. ''But we have to stop at the general store before we see Robbie.'' She flashed him a mischievous grin. ''I want to get a great big bow to tie around your head. Robbie told Santa all he wanted for Christmas was you as his dad. Boy, is Santa ever going to be a hero around our house.''

*   *   *   *   *

SILHOUETTE
DESIRE
®

AVAILABLE FROM 21ST JANUARY 2000

PRINCE CHARMING'S CHILD Jennifer Greene

Man of the Month

With a baby on the way Nicole and Mitch decide to tie the knot. But although it's a marriage of convenience, passion is sizzling beneath the surface…

JUST MY JOE Joan Elliott Pickart

He was tall, dark, drop-dead gorgeous and well out of Polly Chapman's league. Born with a silver spoon in his mouth, he wasn't a man she could just walk away from; Joe was her dream come true…

THE SOLITARY SHEIKH Alexandra Sellers

Sons of the Desert

Powerful Prince Omar desperately desired Jana Stewart, his daughters' tutor, but he resisted her, believing her love was no more than a mirage…

COLONEL DADDY Maureen Child

Bachelor Battalion

When Major Kate Jennings discovered she was pregnant, she was sure the handsome marine with whom she'd been having a passionate affair would propose. But she wanted him to marry her because he loved her!

THE OUTLAW JESSE JAMES Cindy Gerard

Outlaw Hearts

Jesse James had never had time in his life for love. Then in walked Sloan Gantry, knocking his feet out from under him. But this single mum wanted more than just a passionate fling…

COWBOYS, BABIES AND SHOTGUN VOWS
Shirley Rogers

Rugged Ryder McCall was everything virginal Ashley Bennett had ever wanted in a man. But nine months later, married for the sake of their twins, would wedded bliss follow the 'I do'?

Look out in April 2000 for

A Fortune's Children Wedding

and the first book of a 5 part series

The Fortune's Children Brides

2 FREE

books and a surprise gift!

We would like to take this opportunity to thank you for reading this Silhouette® book by offering you the chance to take TWO more specially selected titles from the Desire™ series absolutely FREE! We're also making this offer to introduce you to the benefits of the Reader Service™—

- ★ FREE home delivery
- ★ FREE gifts and competitions
- ★ FREE monthly Newsletter
- ★ Exclusive Reader Service discounts
- ★ Books available before they're in the shops

Accepting these FREE books and gift places you under no obligation to buy, you may cancel at any time, even after receiving your free shipment. Simply complete your details below and return the entire page to the address below. *You don't even need a stamp!*

YES! Please send me 2 free Desire books and a surprise gift. I understand that unless you hear from me, I will receive 4 superb new titles every month for just £2.70 each, postage and packing free. I am under no obligation to purchase any books and may cancel my subscription at any time. The free books and gift will be mine to keep in any case.

D0EA

Ms/Mrs/Miss/Mr ....Initials.................................
BLOCK CAPITALS PLEASE

Surname ....

Address ....

....

....Postcode...................................

Send this whole page to:
UK: FREEPOST CN81, Croydon, CR9 3WZ
EIRE: PO Box 4546, Kilcock, County Kildare (stamp required)